KRA

KRA

by Aguidon

Written and produced in the Netherlands

Foreword with this first edition of KRA

While my original intentions were to create an animated movie, the storyline of this novel already developed early in 2013. However, as the tale became more elaborate within my mind, I realized that my high demands, the atmosphere I required the imagery to breath out, many technical issues, and lack of experience and resources all would make it impossible for me to make such a film in my lifetime, on my own.

At that point I decided to write the script so that it is readable like a book. Although my native language is Dutch, I challenged myself to use the English language. When I finally started writing this book in the second half of 2014, it became one big, intense, life-altering rush until I finished it in the late spring of 2015.

My humble ambitions beyond this first edition are that the book will find its way to a publisher who can publish it in many languages and distribute it all over the world. But a main objective is still to have a film created based on this novel, preferably with human actors.

I have chosen not to use any form of conversation in the book, and thus in a film, there would be yelling, whispering, crisp sound, magnificent music and such, but there would not be any dialogue in any language.

Consequently, a film would not require any subtitling and could therefore be seen, heard and understood by a grandmother in South Africa just as well as a young child somewhere in north Alaska. It would be without any borders.

Aguidon
March 2015

Novel, photo, images, cover design and layout by Aguidon

Thanks to Robin Tanahatoe for reviewing and
Maria Jennings-Kamphuis for all corrections, editing and remarks

Published by Aguidon

Novel / Drama / Adventure

Suitable for all ages
NUR 334

This first edition is cataloged by
Bureau ISBN in the Netherlands.
ISBN 978-90-823-5780-6

This will also be available as an EBook in time.

www.aguidon.com

In remembrance of Kareltje, the young, wild, blue-eyed rook that visited me so many times during the summer of 2005.

Contents

Naming etymology

Kanoa (Male)   Native American name meaning **Free one**

An-Zhi-Mu (Female) Chinese meaning **Peace - Wisdom - Admired**

Keiji (Male)   Japanese name meaning **Lead cautiously**

Luzette (Female)   Spanish name meaning **Light**

Bo (Female/Male)   Chinese name meaning **Precious**

Zuberi (Male)   African name meaning **Strong**

Eadwin (Male)   English name meaning **Valued**

Baaqir (Male)   Arabic Name Meaning **Deeply learned**

Nabhitha (Female)   Indian name meaning **Fearless**

Kra

In old Akan spirituality, the Kra is the **soul** of a person.
It is of divine origin, one gets their Kra from God.

What one chooses to do with this gift in life
determines the meaning and value of one's Kra.

1. Dawn

It is the point of night when the dark quietness is slightly broken by the first sounds of a new day to come. There is a distant sound of flowing water and a far-off rustling noise of formerly green leaves softly crackling in a barely noticeable wind. A fly is buzzing, and a bird can be heard chirping faintly through the far-away groaning of old trees.
Above the horizon in the dark western sky, only the lower right quarter of the moon is shining bright. But its immense appearance, surrounded by a vague aura of morning fog, seems just moments away from plunging into the forests and mountains beneath it.
Far away on a treeless top of one of those mountains, the faint silhouette of a large castle appears.

A few rooks silently fly southwards through the moonlight.
One rook sits on an upper branch of an old, dead weeping willow tree. This old willow hangs a bit askew over the stream, covered by a soft blanket of fog.
The curved and weathered roots of the willow tree are barely visible, just a little bit uphill beyond the reeds and grasses. The ground under the tree is covered with fallen leaves.
Piles of stones and a few boulders are scattered over the hillside.

The young rook has striking blue eyes which look around restlessly. A little fly arouses its curiosity and, as it tries to pick the fly out of the air, the young rook loses its balance.
Almost stumbling off the branch, the rook spreads its wings and flies down in order to land on a rock at the edge of the stream.
A little confused, the rook shakes its feathers and looks around. The fly it tried to catch seems to have vanished.

Glancing around, something else draws the attention of the rook. A large dragonfly is flying by and irregularly twisting itself through the air. As it flies along the reeds, it turns a few times around another rock along the bank and then flies away over the water.

Close to that rock, beneath the water, a golden brown fish restlessly circles around and occasionally seems to nibble at the surface of the water, creating small, circular ripples.

On a crooked reed, a little above that rock, moves a larva or maggot of some kind. That is obviously what the fish is looking at and craving.

All of a sudden, the big dragonfly returns and lands on the same crooked reed. Another dragonfly comes by and the big dragonfly jumps off the reed and flies after it.

Subsequently, the crooked reed moves, which causes the maggot to fall. The maggot lands on the edge of the rock and barely manages to keep itself from falling into the water.

The fish instantly begins swimming back and forth, waiting for breakfast to fall into its already open mouth.

But just when the water's surface is disturbed by the fish's mouth, a curious bird lands in the tree above the rock.

The rook looks up and notices the yellowish bird.

The maggot is incapable of climbing the rock and starts falling, sluggishly rolling over the side of the steep rock, towards the water and the fish's open mouth above the surface.

Then, all of a sudden, the yellow bird flies to the edge of the rock and leans down to look at the maggot, which is just out of reach. It then spreads its wings, flies up and turns around, while its flapping wings disturb the water.

It snatches the maggot with its beak, flies off and lands under the old, dead willow tree, out of which the rook just fell.

The fish angrily swims to deeper waters. The bird places the maggot on another rock near the waterside, chirps a few times and then flies away.

The rook curiously hops to a different rock and sees a small, young and more brownish bird approaching the maggot as its mother flies off to look for more food for the youngster.
While the young bird hops toward the rock, the rook notices an owl sitting on a large tree stump further away. This owl is closely watching the little bird, which is now trying to half jump and half fly onto the rock.
When the little bird finally manages to get onto the rock it hops toward the maggot with its wings dragging a little low.

The rook sees the owl stretch out, stoop down and spread its wings. In a tree close by, a few startled birds noisily fly up to other trees. The rook anxiously looks at the young bird and shrieks loudly. But the young bird has finally reached its destination and starts pecking at the maggot.
As it turns to the owl, the young rook beholds the enormous wings of the predator closing in, without a sound, floating through the air, to grasp its prey.
Again, the rook shrieks to the little bird and jumps closer to the rock where it is still tackling the maggot. The maggot seems too big for the little bird's beak and it keeps dragging it and pecking at it, unaware of the approaching danger.

Seeing the owl closing in and opening its claws, the rook crows loudly, jumps up and spreads its wings. The young rook flies straight towards the rock and, just above the little bird, it lowers its head, folds its wings, and loudly shrieks while it dives straight toward the owl.
The rook hits the side of the owl, which is thrown off balance and needs to use all of its wings' force to prevent it from gliding into the water. One wing sweeps over the rock and knocks the little bird to the ground.
Fluttering over the ground as well, the rook comes to a stop, hops onto a small boulder and crows softly.

The owl flies back to the tree stump. It settles in, turns its head left, then right and finally closes its eyes. With the night almost over, it is time for the owl to sleep.

As the rook inquisitively hops closer to the little bird on the ground, the mother bird lands on the rock and looks down at her unharmed youngster, still pecking at the maggot. She then flies down to it, looks up at the rook and chirps. The rook turns its head a bit askew and seems to nod.
The little bird has finally managed to swallow the maggot and looks up at its mother as if nothing happened.
Once again the mother bird chirps and glances at the rook before she flies towards a nearby tree, followed by her little youngster, fluttering twice as fast to keep up.

The rook now curiously picks at the ground under the old tree. It begins tugging and digging. Its beak rummages through the soil. Pieces of dirt, leaves, even some black feathers and tiny sticks, are moved aside.
Suddenly several rooks fly above the old tree. Two of them crow loudly and land in the tree. The blue-eyed young rook looks up, crows softly and continues pecking and searching in the ground. This seems to upset the older rooks, one of which lands on the ground and crows restlessly again. When this does not seem to bother the young rook that is still searching in the ground, the older rook pecks the neck of the younger rook. The young blue-eyed rook responds with a short cry but still continues what it is doing.

Obviously annoyed, the older rook crows a few times again and flies back into the tree. In the sky, the other rooks fly further south. The second rook now leaves the tree and flies off with the others to the south. The older rook flies down to the ground again. It hops and crows around the young rook, which just looks up for a moment and then continues searching in the ground. With a loud shriek, the older rook flies up, circles around and crows a few times more before following the other rooks flying south.
It seems the young rook has finally found something. Its beak is pulling and wiggling something that appears to be stuck in a lump of dirt.
With its beak in the ground, the rook shakes its head. Dirt, leaves, and twigs are pushed to the side.

The moon and stars are slowly fading in the increasing clarity of the rising sun. The first streaks of sunlight gently fall in long, lingering rays over the slightly vanishing mist, exposing the hazy surroundings.
Then suddenly the rook hops up with something it has pulled out of the ground. With a sense of contentment, the young rook shakes itself.
With something in its beak, it flies up to a branch in the old willow tree. It wipes its beak a few times along the branch to clean it off. Softly crowing, the blue-eyed rook holds its beak up high. The first sunbeams shine straight through a small orb that the rook is proudly holding in its beak. It is like a marble, black yet transparent and shiny.

With the marble clamped in its beak, the rook is still able to crow proudly. Then the rook crouches down and spreads its wings. It flies up above the misty stream and the hazy meadows, viewing the grass, plants, a path running alongside the stream, and the ruins of a tower nearby. The rook flies over the hills, the trees, and a cottage. There is a village to the east and some high mountains beyond. To the north there are grey hills and snowy mountain peaks in the distance. The castle is on the top of the highest mountain beyond the forests to the west.

This magnificent view, the rising sun and the discovery of the fantastic black marble makes the young rook careless with joy. Suddenly, the older rook returns from the south and flies directly towards the young rook, still floating through the sky. Seeing the shiny black marble makes the older rook even more envious and angry than before.
High in the early morning sky, it attacks the young rook from above with a loud, eerie shriek.
Feeling the claws of the elder rook suddenly pinching into its back, the young rook screeches so loud that the silence afterward seems almost frightening.
Between the stream and the path to the village in the east are the ruins of an old tower.

Out of sight in these ruins, a teenage boy, covered in a cape is sleeping on the ground. He abruptly wakes up when he hears the scream of the rook in the sky and he opens his eyes. In a split second he sits up, blinks his eyes a few times and looks up at the sky.
For a moment, his greenish hazel eyes shine in the early morning sunlight. He squints to see the two rooks falling from the sky. With his right hand he brushes aside some of his slightly messy brownish hair and stretches his hand above his eyebrows to see both rooks fluttering and pecking at each other as they fall.

It looks as if both rooks are desperately trying to prevent each other from somehow taking something out of the air. The boy quickly fetches his bag, sweeps his cape over his back, stretches a moment and starts walking on the path towards the two falling rooks.
At about a tree length above the ground, the larger rook suddenly spreads its wings and glides in a steep curve just above the stream and flies up into the sky, heading south once again.
The little rook is able to spread its wings but falls hard into a bush. It shrieks and rolls on the ground before it comes to a stop against a rock. It then lies still.

Immediately, the boy rushes to the poor animal which is already trying to stand up. When he approaches, the young rook flaps its wings but it lacks the strength to fly.
The young rook looks fearfully at the boy, who then sees its remarkable blue eyes. With a gentle smile he tries to calm the rook, which attempts to stand up and quietly crows.

The boy takes an apple out of his bag, sits down and takes a bite. While chewing, he presents the apple to the injured bird by carefully laying it on the ground in front of the rook, which seems interested in the apple.
When the rook begins to peck hungrily at the apple, the boy smiles and sighs with relief.

The young rook seems to be gradually recovering but is still limping a little. It begins to walk around as if it is searching for something, peeking under leaves and pecking around the stone. The boy is a bit startled and confused by the rook's behavior. He tries to make a sound similar to crowing and softly says "kra".

The rook looks up, turns its head, looks at the boy and waits a second before answering with a soft crowing sound. The boy smiles and cautiously tries to imitate the searching behavior around the rock and bush.
He then suddenly holds up a stick and asks the rook: "Hmm?" The rook looks up, makes a barely noticeable humming kind of sound, and continues its search. The boy now just watches the rook as it sifts through the grass and dirt.

After a while he looks at his fingers while turning his hand, glances at the rook, smiles and bends forward towards the stone to start digging around the edges of the stone. The rook seems interested and hops towards the loosened soil to explore the contents. The rook suddenly crows and picks something out of the dirt.

With the black marble in its beak, it looks at the boy and nods a few times. Then it hops towards him and drops the marble in front of the boy.
The boy's mouth falls open and his eyes gaze alternately at the rook and the marble. His hand gradually moves towards the black marble on the ground.
Before he picks it up between his thumb and index finger, he once again looks at the rook which is pointing its beak repeatedly toward the ground.

The boy carefully lifts up the shiny black marble and holds it in front of the low sun in the east.
Just for a short moment, the comforting early morning sunshine feels like a thin, warm blanket of silk.
But suddenly, a chilly wind from the north rustles through the trees. The boy and the rook look at each other.

When the boy turns to the cloudy sky in the north and looks up at the trees on the hill, he catches a glimpse of the cottage and a woman standing outside some distance in front of it.

2. The Cottage

The woman is looking at the northern clouds and is wearing a shiny blue robe, cape and headscarf. The ends of her scarf swirl slightly in the wind with her long black hair. She looks mysterious to the boy. When he turns his head and looks down after some moments, he seems surprised to find that the rook quickly recovered and able to fly since it is now on top of the rock.

The boy gently repeats "kra" a few times, and his hand softly strokes the rook's neck for a moment. The young rook crows quietly, spreads its wings, bends down and jumps up to fly to the nearest tree. Although the rook was limping a little, the boy is happy to see it can still fly.
A little puzzled, the boy holds the black marble up in one hand and waves goodbye to the rook with his other hand.
The rook crows once more, as if responding, and flies into the cloudless southern sky.
Exactly at the moment the boy turns around to look at the cottage further up the hill once more, the woman there turns around as well and sees the boy, who is still kind of holding up his hands. For a moment it feels as though he turns to stone as their eyes meet. Puzzled and confused, he drops his hands and sees the woman looking at him once more before she enters the cottage.

As the trees slightly rustle, the boy sighs, smiles and softly mumbles "kra" while staring at the black marble in his hand. He holds his head a bit askew, raises his eyebrows and sighs.
The boy pulls himself together, puts the marble in his pocket, gets his bag and takes a deep breath before he cautiously starts walking on the path towards the cottage, which arouses his curiosity.

It is still a bit hazy and he notices some fog still hanging above the water down at the stream, as if it was caught between two fences of reeds.

He walks on and regularly peeks at the cottage between the trees. Although there is no one to see, he bends down sometimes as he tries to conceal himself behind the various trees and foliage alongside the path. As he closes in on the cottage, he is almost crawling through the shrubbery.
In the shadows he looks around and sees the village in the east under the emerging sun. A bit beyond the cottage he can see a dark brown horse with a black mane, a simple wagon and the contours of a cloaked man, working on a piece of land.

The boy turns his head toward the cottage again. He can see an open window near the backdoor. Very carefully he moves towards a bush below the window. The only thing he can hear is the rustling of the leaves and grass, caused by his own movements.
He approaches the bush near the cottage and then squats down underneath the open window. As gently as he can, he slowly lifts up his head.
His hair rises above the windowsill. Then his eyebrows. And just when his eyes can nearly look into the cottage over the edge of the window, a dog in the cottage jumps up to the window and barks loudly.
The boy now stares right into a wide-open, growling mouth full of shiny, wet and threatening teeth.

Immediately, the boy falls back onto the ground. Before he even realizes it, the backdoor of the cottage opens and an intimidating young man rushes out.
The young man appears to be in his early twenties and has long black, tied-back hair. He wears a black headband and a black leather belt with a knife to accentuate his somewhat fearsome appearance. He grabs a shovel and shouts, glaring at the boy.

Completely in shock, the boy remains prostrate on the ground, anxiously watching the dog, which is now barking behind the threatening young man.
Then the boy hears a hushing voice. The dog growls a little and then becomes quiet. Only its agitated breathing remains somewhat loud.
The young man glances at the door, as a girl, a few years older than the boy on the ground, comes walking out. As she bends down and kneels alongside the dog, her long brown hair drapes over the dog's back.

While her hand caresses the animal's head a little, her soothing voice calms the dog till its tail wags gently.
The girl stands up and looks at the young man, blinking her eyes slowly to tranquilize the atmosphere. And then she looks at the boy.
Still startled and frightened but nervously sitting up, the boy looks at her and detects a friendly smile on her face. His eyes grow large for a moment when he looks into her sympathetic brown eyes.
The older girl gestures for the boy to stand up. He stands up and wipes his clothes a few times. While looking up, he watches the girl as she tries to guide the young man inside.
But the young man waits at the door until the girl and the dog enter the cottage.

With his head bent down a little, the boy passes the young man, who stares at him and puts down the shovel quite loudly. The boy glances at the horse in front of the barn, looks up at the young man and walks a few steps inside.
The boy takes in the cozy and simple interior. He notes that the dog now lies in the corner but looking more carefully, he sees that it is lying near a large basket in which there are two other young dogs.
They are brown, black and white, like the mother. Then he sees that there is also a solid black one sitting outside the basket.
When the young black dog tries to join the others in the basket, they snarl and growl at it.

The cottage has wooden walls and a stone floor. Its simple furnishings consist of a table, a few chairs, a chest, a closet, a few shelves, some capes and cloaks hanging on the wall, and a sword above the entrance. A stove against the wall casts a warm orange light onto the floor.

The girl whispers something to the young man and walks to another room in the back. The young man takes a chair and sits down.

He leans his elbows on the table and he gestures to the boy to take a chair and sit down as well. The boy quietly puts down his bag, removes his cape, pulls out a chair and calmly sits down.

The little black dog sits up and curiously walks towards the boy. It first sniffs the bag and then the boy's leg before it looks up at the boy with its big, light-blue eyes.

This instantly reminds the boy of the friendly, blue-eyed young rook from which he got the black marble.

While the young man across the table begins to show something that looks a little like a smile, the boy gently reaches out to the little dog with one hand, while his other hand grasps in his pocket to fetch the black marble.

The little dog howls softly as it leans on the boy's legs and wags its tail. With one hand he helps the little animal onto his lap. He slowly moves his other hand above the table.

He does not want to show his marble but only wants to take a peek. He slightly opens his hand a little bit just above the table.

The young man observes this. His eyes slightly squint as if he suspects that there is something in the boy's hand.

When the girl walks in with a wooden tray in her hand, the young man pays no further attention to the boy. Therefore the boy opens his hand just a bit more and finds himself looking at his marvelous little marble.

The girl gives a steaming mug to the young man, puts two more mugs on the table and, with a brief, soft hum, she presents the last mug to the boy, who looks at the dog on his lap.

As he looks up and tries to grab the mug, however, the dog tries to climb up onto the table. Reflexively, the boy moves both hands to make the dog sit back on his lap. In doing so he jostles the mug and spills some hot tea on his hand.

"Ahh!" he exclaims, and immediately pulls his hand away, letting the marble fall out of his hand. It bounces over the table a few times before it rolls over the edge and subsequently bounces a few times on the ground before it rolls further across the floor.

While the girl softly wipes the tea off the table with the cloth she had over her arm, she looks at the boy and then swiftly, but very gently, wipes the remaining drops of tea off the boy's empty hand.

The boy smiles shyly while he keeps staring at the black marble rolling on the ground. The young man sits up and follows the marble's path with a thunderstruck expression on his face. His obviously startled behavior makes the girl turn around. They all see the marble come to a stop under the slipper of someone who has just come from the other room. As the boy looks up, he can see the silky blue robe, the slim stature and the headscarf. He realizes that this is the mysterious lady he saw outside from a distance earlier.

There is a moment of silence as they all tensely gaze at the marble. It seems like everything has come to a standstill and then gradually starts up again. The lady quietly bends down and picks up the marble very carefully. She meticulously keeps her dark-brown eyes focused on it while she stands up and walks to the table.

The silence is only broken by the few tiny creaks and squeaks of the wooden floor as the lady slowly steps toward the table.

The young man stands up and assists her with her chair as the lady sits down. As if she were in a kind of trance, she cautiously puts the marble in the center of the table, sits back, and takes a deep breath.

While exhaling, the seriousness on her face finally makes room for a subdued smile. She then slightly turns her head askew and looks at the boy.
Once again, there is a serene, somewhat tense, silence. The boy looks at the marble on the table, turns to the young man, to the lady and the girl next to him.
The girl, or young lady, who seems a few years younger than the man, breaks the tension by moving her hands to her chest, and saying "Luzette" and smiling.
A little shy and insecure, the teenage boy moves one hand to his chest, softly clears his throat and says "Kanoa".
The young man respectfully stands up, moves his hand to his chest, pronounces "Keiji", nods and sits down again.

After a short silence, Kanoa looks at the lady, who remains silent. Luzette then bends her hand towards the lady and says "AnZhiMu". The lady smiles a bit, gently runs one hand over Kanoa's hair and briefly puts her hand on the boy's shoulder while she looks him straight in the eyes.

The little black dog on Kanoa's lap snores softly a few times. AnZhiMu then looks at the marble, sits back, bows her head a little and then looks at Kanoa again.
Although the boy is staring at the black marble on the table, he feels all eyes are on him.
Kanoa picks up the marble, takes a deep breath, moves his chair, carefully lifts the little black dog to the floor and stands up.
He walks a bit to the window, and points outside toward the place where he found the marble. The little black dog follows him to the window with a wagging tail.

To explain what happened there, Kanoa first lays his head on his hands and closes his eyes. Then he screams "kra, kra", opens his eyes, and points to the sky.
With both hands he indicates two birds falling, fighting, flapping and fluttering until his hands are low above the floor. Then he lets one hand skim the floor, fly away and vanish into the sky.

While he pronounces "kra, kra" once more, the other hand falls onto the floor and rolls a little before it comes to a stop. Luzette and Keiji observe the boy with rapt attention. In the meantime, AnZhiMu covers her mouth with her hand and anxiously watches Kanoa's portrayal very attentively.

Kanoa's hand now imitates a recovering bird, briefly caressed by his other hand. He then points both index fingers to his eyes and subsequently points them to the young dog's blue eyes to indicate the bright blue color of the bird's eyes.
He continues with his hand on the ground, pretending that it is his friendly young rook, which clearly seems to be searching for something. He kneels down and pretends to search in the ground himself as well.
When he mimes the bird finding something, he shows the marble between his fingers.

AnZhiMu has both hands before her mouth now. Luzette has laced her fingers together tightly. Keiji's mouth hangs a bit open while he watches Kanoa explain how he got the marble. Kanoa concludes with another "kra" as he lets one hand slowly fly up while holding the marble in the other hand before placing it back on the table again.
Kanoa now sees the impact this story has made on the others. Even the dogs are completely still.

The silence is broken by the sliding of the chair which Kanoa pulls back. As he sits down, the boy notices Keiji nodding.
The black dog jumps against Kanoa's leg and he helps it climb onto his lap once more. He looks briefly into the animal's eyes and tickles it a little.
He then fetches his mug and softly slurps his tea. He gently places it back on the table and looks up. The others seem stunned by his story.

AnZhiMu now reaches out one hand to the marble, pauses and looks at Kanoa questioningly. Kanoa nods his approval. Luzette and Keiji watch with wide eyes as AnZhiMu picks up the marble.

She holds it up against the window's light and stares at it for some time. When she lays it back on the table, Luzette and Keiji both look at her very anxiously.
AnZhiMu takes a deep breath and sighs slowly. She takes a sip of her tea, stands up, looks at Keiji for a short moment and slowly walks to the other room. Keiji stands up immediately and follows her.
Kanoa raises his eyebrows and briefly looks at Luzette. She is obviously a little upset but she tries to smile.
Kanoa gently pets the little black dog on his lap. It looks up and whimpers softly before it lays its head down again and closes its eyes. A little timid, Kanoa smiles back at Luzette but then he is suddenly startled by Keiji striding back into the room.

With a determined pace Keiji goes to the door, stretches up and takes down the big sword that was mounted above it.
He puts the sword on his belt, grabs a black cape hanging on one of the hooks besides the door and throws it over his shoulders. Although he is fairly thin, his serious expression, long black hair, headband, sword and cape all make Keiji look like a warrior.

3. The Village

AnZhiMu comes back into the room and restlessly walks to the door to fetch her cape. While she puts it on, she looks at Luzette, who stands up and assists her with the cape. Luzette is whispering softly while Kanoa places the little black dog on the ground and stands up as well.

Just as he is about to pick up the marble from the table, AnZhiMu steps towards him, softly takes his hand and looks at him in a soothing way. She picks up the marble herself and puts it in a small pocket in her robe.

Kanoa questioningly looks at Luzette, who nods approvingly.

Keiji has already opened the door and is walking outside. AnZhiMu follows him as he walks to the horse. Just before he jumps on the horse in one swift movement, AnZhiMu briefly reaches out her hand.

While Keiji softly strokes the dark brown horse's head, he looks at the others for a moment. Then he turns his head, sits up, takes the reins and quickly rides off down the hill and then to the west. AnZhiMu waves goodbye with one arm stretched towards Keiji's path, as if her hand waves to the mountains and the castle ahead. She holds her other hand anxiously over her mouth.

When she turns around, she points at the cloaked figure still working in the field, looks at Luzette and briefly takes the girl's hand. She glances toward Kanoa and then hastily walks in the direction of the village to the east.

After AnZhiMu has disappeared behind the trees along the path, Luzette looks at Kanoa and then toward the cloaked figure. Having obviously noticed Keiji hastily riding away to the west and AnZhiMu leaving for the village in a hurry, he places his hoe against a tree and begins walking towards the cottage.

"Zuberi", Luzette shouts. As she walks towards him, she jovially, yet gently, pulls Kanoa's arm to have him follow her.

Kanoa is rather reluctant however because he seems a little intimidated by Zuberi's quite large stature, his dark cape and the hood which hides most of his face.
Luzette walks to Zuberi, lays one hand on his forearm and points at Kanoa and mentions his name. They whisper for a moment before they both walk towards Kanoa.

While Luzette happily rushes back towards the cottage, Kanoa looks a bit shy and confused. As Zuberi passes him, he bows briefly. Kanoa, still not able to see his face, nods and follows them into the cottage.
Luzette quickly removes AnZhiMu's mug and presents the still untouched mug of Keiji to Zuberi, who now slowly pulls back the hood of his cloak.

When Kanoa sits down at the table, the little black dog, which has been following him all the time, once again begs to sit on his lap. As he places the animal onto his lap, Kanoa looks up and can scarcely behold the disfigured face of Zuberi, now sitting in front of him.
He seems about the same age as Keiji. He has friendly, dark-brown eyes and short, curly, black hair but there is a large protrusion right above his nose on his forehead.
This strange malformation, combined with his pronounced chin, makes him look rather frightening.
Kanoa's shock makes the little dog on his lap restless too and it tries to climb up on the table. When Zuberi reaches out his hand, the dog licks it.
After a short caress, Zuberi smiles and retracts his hand to fetch the mug. Feeling that it is not hot tea anymore, he drinks the whole mug empty in one gulp. As he slowly places the mug back on the table, he notices Kanoa staring at him. They both smile, slightly embarrassed, and look down. Kanoa seems to understand that although Zuberi looks quite scary, he seems to be a kind young man.

While the young Kanoa softly pets the little dog on his lap, he watches Luzette and Zuberi stand up and walk outside, where Luzette appears to explain the story to Zuberi.
Kanoa decides to go outside as well and, naturally, the young black dog promptly follows him again.
When he steps over the threshold, he notices Zuberi looking at him intrigued and even bowing a little towards him, it seems.

Luzette smiles at Kanoa and nudges Zuberi in his side. He looks at her and she nods. Now Zuberi moves both hands to his mouth to form a kind of horn.
He walks a few steps in the direction of the village to the east and starts uttering strange and surprisingly loud sounds like "Owwhha, HopHop, PrrrwAh" and so on.
It is so loud that some startled birds fly out of a tree further away. After a few moments and breaths, he yells the same sounds into the sky once more.
Not long after he finishes, he cautiously and silently walks back to Luzette. As they look at the village in the east, both Zuberi and Luzette seem to be waiting for something.

After a few serene moments a faint shout suddenly seems to drop out of the sky. Luzette and Zuberi briefly look at each other and then Zuberi steps towards the east again, turns his head askew, listens and waits.
Then a song of strange sounds comes swirling out of the air. It is similar to what Zuberi yelled, but with a lower pitch. Kanoa is amazed by the song's tones which echo through the air. Zuberi then responds with a few short yells and turns back to the cottage, followed by Luzette.
Kanoa is intrigued and remains outside while he stares into the trees and far off into the sky.
He hears a shriek somewhere above and then sees a hawk descending into the village.

The boy cannot see that this hawk flies over the village wall and lands on the outstretched arm of a figure standing hidden in the shadows of the old wall.

It is a man in old robes and a dark and dirty cape that hides the walking stick he is leaning on. He turns his head and looks at the hawk, revealing a sinister face that would make anyone uneasy.

While Kanoa is looking around in the trees, he suddenly hears a crowing sound. He turns his head and carefully listens to the trees, eagerly looking around.
He softly calls "Kra" a few times and waits. And then, as he had hoped, all of a sudden he sees Kra flying into the nearest tree.
With a delighted smile on his face, he walks towards the tree, reaches out his hand and looks at the young rook.
Kra steps left and right on the branch a few times. Then the rook spreads its wings and glides over Kanoa's arm to land on his shoulder. With a delighted smile Kanoa walks to a large stone nearby and sits down on it.

The little black dog shows its excitement by wagging its tail and joyfully jumping around the boy. Kanoa gently raises his finger to play with the rook's beak and he softly strokes its neck, while looking at its innocent, light-blue eyes.

Luzette and Zuberi both stand in the doorway of the cottage. Astonished by the sight of the boy, the rook and the dog, Luzette puts her hands over her mouth and looks at Zuberi with a somewhat nervous smile.
She then points at the rook on Kanoa's shoulder and asks Kanoa, "Kra?" Kanoa nods and pets the rook. Luzette and Zuberi restlessly gesture and whisper as they walk towards Kanoa. Zuberi is obviously preparing for something.

He sighs, tightens his cape and looks far to the south. He steps toward Kanoa, takes his hand, encloses it within his other hand, and firmly shakes it while humbly looking down.
When he releases Kanoa's hand, he looks at Luzette and then starts walking towards the south. As soon as Zuberi is down the hill, he starts running.

After Kanoa and Luzette see him vanish into the morning haze, Luzette points at the village in the east. She briefly puts her hand on Kanoa's chest and then on her own chest and points at the village again. It is obvious she wants them to follow AnZhiMu and go to the village together.

In the meantime, AnZhiMu is already entering the village. The path has become a street as she hastily walks past the first houses and market stalls. One hand holds her cape around her neck while the other hand discretely hides the pocket containing the black marble.
As she walks past a few parked wagons, she looks up at a higher part of the village where a few yellow-brown stone houses, constructed on top of an old piece of the village wall, catch her eye. In them are deep holes that appear to be windows, making the houses look a bit mysterious. AnZhiMu moves on, passing various men, women and children.
As the street climbs higher, it also gets narrower. When AnZhiMu has reached the other side of the village, she stops before a somewhat rounded and eroded stairway along the village wall.
She looks up at a heavy, old, wooden door that seems to be sunken into the wall at the top of the stairway above. She places her right foot onto the first step.

Meanwhile, Keiji is passing a few farms and houses galloping along the path. Further up, between the many trees on the mountainside, the castle is now clearly visible on top of the mountain in front of him.
The low, bright sunlight shining through the trees makes the sweaty coat of the rapidly moving horse shine.

Zuberi has now reached a more desert-like terrain in the south. He stops and yells "HopHop" in a high-pitched voice.
After some time, two camels come galloping toward him.
When they stop in front of him, one of them utters a deep rattling moan. Zuberi runs his hand along the neck and the back of one animal. It bends its forelegs and that is enough for Zuberi to jump onto its back.

The camel slowly stands back up again. Zuberi whispers a command and moves his hands along the camel's neck.
The camels start walking further south and within a few moments Zuberi and the camels are just slightly visible as a dusty cloud along the south horizon.

Luzette and Kanoa go into the cottage to prepare for the walk to the village.
While Kanoa gently strokes Kra, the friendly young rook still on his shoulder, Luzette cleans up the mugs and walks to the other room. When she returns, she briefly pets the mother dog in the basket. With the other two pups sleeping against her belly, the dog looks up and rests her head again as Luzette whispers a few things to her.
Luzette now walks towards the door and takes her shawl from the wall. This makes Kanoa consider taking his bag and cape, but when he starts to pick them up, Luzette gently shakes her head. Kanoa understands that they will return here later.

With Kra on his shoulder and the little black dog still walking and jumping around him, Kanoa remains a bit behind Luzette as they start the short journey to the village beneath the bright sun in the east.

As they walk into the village, Kanoa curiously looks around at the various houses, and shops and people he notices.
There is a group of men wearing headscarves, a few older men with long robes and turbans on their heads, and women and children in colorful clothing.
The fact that some people seem to be staring at Kanoa and whispering makes him feel uneasy but he is comforted by the joyful presence of the rook and the dog.
Luzette looks back at him with a somewhat suppressed smile every now and then as they walk the same path that AnZhiMu took earlier.

With the hawk on his shoulder, the sinister man in the dark, dirty cape is on the other side of the street.

As he tries to hide himself behind the corner of a house, he stares malevolently at the boy, the girl, the rook and the dog.

When Luzette sets her foot on the first step of the eroded stairway towards the sunken wooden door above, through which AnZhiMu entered earlier, the little black dog barks and starts climbing the stairs.
After a smooth glide, Kra flies up and lands on a stone handrail near the door. Just as Luzette raises her hand to knock on the door, it clicks and slowly, with a crackle and a crunch, it slides open. Kra hops, turns and looks at the door.
Slightly startled, Luzette steps back and turns her head to see Kanoa mounting the last steps and curiously watching the opening door. The young dog nosily sniffs around.

Keiji has arrived at the top of the mountain and is now slowly riding towards the castle. The path widens and there are fewer trees around. While he keeps looking straight forward toward the gate, the few people on the roadside look up and whisper as they see him.
He stops his horse at the gate before two guards and softly strokes its neck just below the black mane of the animal. He says "Eadwin" and then sits up and waits.

The guards look at each other seriously, but also quite questioningly, and seem to have no intention to move aside.
Keiji utters the name of Eadwin again, a bit louder, and then, after another breath, also says "AnZhiMu". This makes the guards move aside straight away.

Keiji slowly rides through the gate. He is sitting straight up and stoically keeps his eyes focused on the main entrance.
The people in the courtyard notice Keiji. There are several guards and knight-like figures, as well as horses, stables, noblemen and noblewomen, workmen, maids and also some children. They all look up to see him approaching the main building.

They watch him step off his horse and lead it to a drinking trough, whispering and gently rubbing its back for a brief moment.

Then, as Keiji walks towards the entrance, he can vaguely hear people talking inside. Before he can climb the last few steps leading to the large entrance, he is stopped by two guards once again. He promptly says "Eadwin, AnZhiMu". Both guards step aside and Keiji walks up the stairs.

At the entrance, just in front of two huge and intricately carved wooden doors, Keiji pauses, takes a deep breath, and stretches both arms toward the doors.

He waits just a moment before he pushes both doors open and steps into the immense and majestic hall. At the end of the hall King Eadwin sits on his throne, surrounded by many nobles, gentlefolk, servants, guards and a minstrel of some kind.

A few guards instantly grab for their swords as they see Keiji enter. But King Eadwin has them put down their arms with a simple wave of his hand.

While everyone silently watches Keiji walking to the king, the tension is gradually broken by an increasing smile on King Eadwin's face.

One of the king's light-brown, slightly graying curls falls in front of his bright blue eyes for a moment. He brushes it aside as he stands up, tilts his head and opens his arms to embrace Keiji. He seems surprised and happy to see Keiji, who is evidently relieved to see that the king remembers him.

When he sees the serious look in Keiji's eyes, he waves the surrounding attendees to stay back or leave.

He also gestures to an attendant to bring Keiji something to eat and drink. Then he fetches his cup and sits down at the end of a long rectangular wooden table.

As it empties, the hall gradually becomes a large, serene and reverberant space. Keiji, the king and two of his closest advisors sit at the table together.

The minstrel steps towards Keiji, bows, and is obviously allowed to remain with the king and his company.

Meanwhile, Kanoa and Luzette stand in front of the slowly opening door to see a thin, dark figure emerge.
Luzette quickly bows, turns to the boy and moves her hand toward Kanoa while she states his name. She then moves her hand towards the old man in the doorway and says "Baaqir".
As the door is now fully open, Kanoa sees a gentle man with thin grey hair smiling at him.
Kra jumps back onto Kanoa's shoulder and Baaqir says "oooh" when he sees the friendly blue-eyed rook. Then he bows slightly and invites them all into his house with a sweeping gesture of his hand.

The little black dog has already entered the house and runs to AnZhiMu, who is sitting on an old chair between a wooden table and a fireplace.
It is quite dark and somewhat dusty in the room, which is filled with all kinds of stuff. There are books, chests of all sizes, shelves, bottles, small statues, candles, a long pipe, maps, documents and, on the table, close to an old book of some kind, is the black marble, which has just been picked up by AnZhiMu.

Kra immediately notices the black marble it discovered this morning and flies up to land on the edge of the table. It turns its head and looks at the marble with curiosity.
Surprised and amused, AnZhiMu moves the marble slowly and carefully in front of the rook.
The rook picks it up, starts to nod and joyfully steps back and forth a few times.
Once again, Baaqir says "ooh", expressing his astonishment. He slowly sits down, keeping his eyes fixed on the rook proudly holding the marble in its beak.
With his hand, Baaqir mimics a bird on the table. His index finger acts like a beak, pecking and ticking on the wooden table.

Kra seems interested and hops towards Baaqir's hand, making it possible for the man to gently tickle the frisky rook's neck.
Baaqir's soft, friendly laughter is replaced by the creaking of his wooden chair as he slowly sits back down.

Luzette is already sitting in front of the fireplace. Baaqir gestures for Kanoa to take a stool and sit down at the table as well.
As the old man sits up and opens the very old and very large book on the table, he briefly looks at AnZhiMu, who watches attentively. Kra hops to the side of the table where Kanoa sits down. Baaqir mumbles softly as he cautiously browses through the loose pages of the old book, which seems to be a collection of various kinds of ancient drawings.

The rook now nods up and down with the marble still in its beak as if it wants to release the marble. Kanoa raises his hand to the rook.
The palm of his hand is hardly open when Kra drops the black marble into it. As he looks at the shiny little black ball in his hand closely, he can see the others motionlessly staring in the reflection of this marvelous marble.

Kra crows softly and flies up to the window in the deep stone wall and starts arranging its feathers, as all birds do.
Baaqir seems to have found something because he explicitly points at a drawing, repeatedly utters a low "hmm" and alternately looks at Kanoa, AnZhiMu and the drawing on the document in the book while he nods regularly.
Kanoa is very surprised to see an ancient ink drawing on parchment that shows a rook, just below a crown, with a marble in its upraised beak. Besides some irregular wear and tear at the edges, the drawing shows two dissimilar sides on the bottom half of the page below the rook.
On the right, there is a landscape with many trees, cattle, farmlands, villages, mountains and a castle. Kanoa seems to recognize some things in this image somehow as he squints his eyes and looks more closely for a moment.

On the left side, the drawing shows harsh mountains, dead trees and dark clouds above partially burnt fields and wastelands.

The room is in complete silence and Baaqir now points right at the eyes of the rook in the drawing. When Kanoa looks closely, he discovers a faded, but clearly visible, blue color in the eyes.
Kanoa turns to the rook in the window and then stares at the marble, still in his hand.

The tense silence is abruptly disturbed by Baaqir, who closes the book and commences to stand up.
Kra turns to Kanoa, crows, and, quickly flies back onto his shoulder. The little dog barks and runs, frisky as ever, to the boy as well. AnZhiMu also stands up.
She and Baaqir communicate in a secretive and whispering way while Luzette approaches the dog and bends down.
Kanoa hears Baaqir speak of Keiji and Eadwin. When Baaqir asks for Zuberi, he and AnZhiMu both questioningly look at Luzette, who stands up quickly and nods approvingly.
They first look at each other for a moment, before the thin, old man slightly bows and embraces the slim and almost fragile lady. When Baaqir walks towards the boy, the little black dog barks at him.
He smiles, bends down and says "Booh" trying to scare the dog in a gentle and funny way. "Bo", Kanoa repeats with a smile and immediately the little black dog looks up at him.
Kanoa puts the marble in his pocket and bends down to caress the dog a little. The serious expressions of the others gradually become smiles.
Kanoa repeats Bo's name once more and bends down. He gently picks up the young dog, holds the animal in his arms and cuddles it with an innocent and happy smile.
Bo enthusiastically licks the boy's face and Kanoa has to lean back, which makes everyone smile.

4. Parting

While Baaqir walks to the door and slowly opens it, AnZhiMu gestures quite explicitly at Luzette. As Kanoa walks outside, through the doorway, Kra flies into the sky.
The rook circles around, crows a few times, and flies off in a southern direction. With his hand still in an upraised waving position, Kanoa stares into the sky and seems to wonder about the meaning of all this. His thoughts are interrupted as Luzette joins him outside.

AnZhiMu seems to be preparing some things before she leaves the house. She and Baaqir wave goodbye to the young boy and girl, who are accompanied by Bo, the little black dog, as they descend the worn stone stairway on their way back to the cottage.

On the opposite side of the road, partially hidden at the top of another stairway, the sinister figure has been watching it all. He ties a tiny roll of parchment onto the leg of the hawk perched on his arm. Then he raises his arm up high and eventually lets the hawk fly. Its shrill, eerie shriek pierces the sky towards its destination to the north.

Just as AnZhiMu is closing the door, she hears the hawk's shriek. She peeks through the small, almost closed, doorway and sees the hawk fly off. When she looks back at where the hawk came from, on the other side of the road, the cloaked figure immediately hides himself.
AnZhiMu stares and hesitates for some moments before she finally closes the door and releases the handle.

Meanwhile, Keiji is preparing to return from the castle. He is not alone as he heads down the mountain.

Riding beside him are the two closest advisors of King Eadwin and a few guards. They all ride at a slow, steady pace. They precede a closed carriage with two white horses. The driver sits up straight and holds the horses' reins while he focuses on the road in front of them. Keiji, somewhat proudly, takes the lead in this small, formal parade, heading towards the cottage.

The sky to the north seems to thicken with clouds. The hawk utters a loud and eerie shriek while it flies below the darkening clouds, over light-grey wastelands and strange rock formations. It heads towards a small, dark forest that lies between steep, rocky hills. The forest is nestled in front of several huge, craggy, snowcapped mountains far to the north.

Gliding, flapping its wings just every now and then, Kra flies to the south. The rook follows Zuberi, who is still riding on a camel over the dunes towards a settlement, which seems to emerge from the bright sunlight further south.

Zuberi sees the first tents appear beyond the hill he climbs. Here the sand and few cactuses gradually make room for more bushes and trees. Between the rocks, shrubbery and trees, a path appears. It leads him downhill toward a small community living in various tents, surrounded by lush green trees. Close to the open central area is a very large tent with an entrance guarded by two men.
Cattle, camels and horses are grazing close to a small lake surrounded by palm trees further downhill. Behind the lake and trees, far in the distance, some steep, rocky hills stand out between the many waves of dunes along the horizon.
Kra lands on a scruffy tree near the edge of the settlement. Only a child notices the rook but he pays no attention and continues playing with the other children.

As AnZhiMu leaves Baaqir's house, she looks up at the other side of the road again but does not see anyone.

She hurries back down through the street market, but she turns her head and looks back every now and then.
While doing so, she trips over some pottery stacked next to a vendor's stall. She manages to stay standing up by grabbing the side of the stall. AnZhiMu apologizes to the vendor, who seems to know her and smiles. While she looks around, she sees the cloaked, sinister figure, who has obviously followed her, disappear around the corner of an alley. She remains at the stall in the street market and asks the vendor something. He offers her a piece of bread and walks into the house behind his stall.

While AnZhiMu waits and looks around, she tries to look relaxed and her hasty movements are replaced by stillness.
She cannot see the sinister man as he secretly moves to another position and spies on her from a shop on the other side of the street.

This cloaked, sinister figure now watches as another lady approaches the vendor's stall. The women whisper, gesture and subsequently enter the vendor's house behind the stall.
The sinister man grumbles and takes an apple out of a basket from a stall close to him.
The vendor behind that stall yells angrily at him but when the cloaked figure turns his face towards the man he immediately falls silent and submissively pretends to be cleaning his stall.
The dark sinister figure looks up and down the street and then, like a turtle, he retreats into his dark cloak's hood. His eyes are now fixated on the other side of the street.
Inside the vendor's house, AnZhiMu gets another brown cape, which she pulls over her own robe.
She leaves the house through the backdoor and takes an alternate route out of the village, heading back to her cottage on the hill.

In the meantime Baaqir has left his house in the village wall and is now at a large barn with a stable, just outside the village.

Near the stable stands a sturdy brown horse with a thick blonde mane.
As Baaqir opens the tall barn doors, it is obvious he suffers from some physical discomfort, caused either by age or past injuries.
When the barn is open, he walks over to the horse near the stable, whispers and gently runs his hand through its mane.

After some time he leads the horse in front of the barn and places a trough filled with hay before the animal.
For quite some time he is busy walking in and out of the barn, picking up items and taking them inside. There are a few gentle neighs from the horse and the constant shuffling and rumbling sound of things being moved within the barn.

After a while, it gradually gets quieter and Baaqir stands near the horse. He caresses the animal and removes the trough.
He carries some ropes out of the barn and attaches them to the horse's harness.
Baaqir then disappears back into the barn and, after some more shuffling, the peaceful silence is disturbed by a shout, which makes the strong horse start pulling something.
It takes an enormous amount of effort to get whatever it is moving. The ropes crackle under the tension. After another shout, and a sudden crack, there is a loud, rumbling sound as the horse slowly starts walking forward.
Gradually a wagon with a small two-story wooden house built on top of it emerges. The house's roof just clears the high doors of the barn.

Although it sounds a bit creaky and looks a bit wobbly because of its height, this piece of craftsmanship is actually a complete little wooden cottage on wheels. It has a door and a little balcony on the back, windows with small shutters on the sides, a second floor with a pointy, tiled roof and a chimney on top.
Almost on the road, Baaqir softly utters "Ho" to make the horse and wagon-house come to a stop. He steps off, walks back to the barn and slowly closes both the high barn doors.

He walks back to the wagon, returns to the driver's seat, and picks up the reins. Baaqir takes a deep breath and, while the strong horse still holds the ropes tight, he shouts, signaling the horse to continue. Once again, the whole structure slowly starts moving. It rumbles and creaks forward and turns onto the road towards the mountains in the west.

When Zuberi enters the settlement, some children make fun of his disfigured face and laugh. Some younger children look up, scream and run away, startled by his appearance.
This commotion alarms several elderly residents. One boy seems especially concerned about Zuberi as he stands still and stares at him on the slowly passing camel.
Suddenly this boy runs across the open central area toward the largest tent, straight ahead of Zuberi. The impressive round tent has vertical sides and an enormous pointy roof. The boy stops before the guards, who both keep their eyes on Zuberi and allow the boy to proceed into the tent.

Kra remains in the tree on the side of the small settlement and seems to take notice of all of this. In front of the large tent's entrance, Zuberi's camel comes to a stop and starts bending its front knees. While Zuberi prepares to dismount, the boy moves aside the colorful curtain of beads hanging in the tent's entrance and comes out of the tent, leading someone else.
The rook flies off, back to the north. No one notices this, however, as everybody is watching Zuberi and what appears to be the leader of the settlement, who is now stepping out of the large tent. The leader walks under the draped, white cloth of the tent's awning. Both guards stand ready as he approaches Zuberi.

Luzette and Kanoa have reached the edge of the village and they quietly continue down the road. Bo walks around them, in front of them and behind them with a wagging tail. It alternates between sniffing alongside the road and looking up at one of them. The innocent looks of the jolly dog bring a smile to their faces every now and then.

As Luzette and the boy proceed further down the path, which winds between various trees and shrubs, Kanoa looks down the hill and sees the stream again. When the path reaches the ruins of the old tower, Kanoa stops.
Bo, who had been running in front of them on the path towards the cottage, immediately runs back to Kanoa and looks where he is looking.
The dog cheerfully runs down the path toward the stream. Kanoa smiles and follows Bo. Luzette first turns her head and then curiously follows the boy and the dog.

The boy stands before the ruins, where he woke up early this morning. His fingers kind of play with his lower lip and he seems to be lost in thought for a while.
Luzette walks towards him and gently disturbs his wandering thoughts by softly touching his arm. Slightly startled, Kanoa looks at her and then points at his sleeping place. Luzette now precedes him into the ruins and curiously looks at the little dog sniffing around the rocks in the ruins. Just as Kanoa turns his head to the spot where he found Kra and the marble, a loud crowing sound echoes through the air.

He looks around and shouts Kra's name. The boy can see the rook flying towards him from the south. Although Kanoa stretches his arm upwards, Kra flies over them and lands in the old willow tree near the stream. It is almost exactly above the spot where it found the marble in the ground very early this morning.

Bo joyfully runs in front of Luzette and Kanoa as they walk down the path towards the stream and the old tree beyond the reeds. As they stand on the path before the dead willow tree on the opposite side of the water, Kanoa looks into the sky in the other direction. Then he looks down at the bush and the stone where he saw Kra fall out of the sky.
In the willow, Kra crows loudly to attract their attention. When they look at the young rook, it flies down to the rock and hops over to the lump of ground under the tree, where it pulled out the marble at dawn.

Kanoa looks puzzled and points at the spot where he met Kra with one hand while he holds the marble up high and clearly visible between two fingers in the other hand.

Kra now hops on the rock, bends down, spreads it wings, and flies just over the water. Then it glides straight towards Kanoa, who is still holding the marble up between his fingers.

As the boy expects Kra to land on his shoulder, he frowns when he sees the rook approaching at a fairly high speed. When Kra flies just over him, Kanoa closes his eyes. The rook plucks the marble out of his fingers and flies high up into the sky. This seems to make Luzette very nervous. She cries out and immediately restrains herself by putting her hand over her mouth. She anxiously follows the rook in the sky with her eyes.

Kanoa is a little startled by the rook's behavior, but he does not seem to mind that it has taken the marble. With a smile on his face and one hand shading his eyes, he watches Kra flying back to the old willow tree on the other side of the stream.

The rook then flies to the spot on the ground where it found the marble, and, with the marble still in its beak, mimes the searching and eventually the finding of the marble.

Kanoa does not understand it and, once again, points at the spot where Kra fell on the ground, on his side of the stream and a bit uphill.

But the young rook crows repeatedly and starts imitating its search under the tree again. After a while, it flies up into the tree, holds its beak up high, and subsequently flies high into the sky. Then suddenly it shrieks and starts fluttering its wings wildly. The rook then seems to fall down but it flaps its wings in time to land on the stone where Kanoa first met Kra. The boy starts to realize that Kra first found the marble near the old willow and later dropped it close to the stone, where he found both the rook and the marble early this morning.

Somewhat astonished, Kanoa and Luzette watch the little dog bark and run off toward the rook.

Luzette looks at Kanoa a little tense, but when she sees the smile on his face her anxiety gradually melts into smile.
As they both start walking over to the rook and the dog, Kanoa looks back at the willow for a moment and smiles.
When Kanoa arrives at the spot where he met the fallen rook earlier, he starts imitating a search.
He gently bends down and lightly ploughs through the loose soil near the stone. Now Kra hops towards his hand, softly crows and points its head upwards while holding the marble in its beak. Kanoa holds up his hand and the little rook drops the marble in his hand again.

With an obvious sigh of relief, Luzette watches the boy receive the marble from the rook. She seems quite afraid of losing the marble and remains a bit puzzled by the whole incident.
But the calm and confident way Kanoa looks at the old tree across the stream shows that he now understands where Kra actually found the marble. Still a bit lost in his thoughts, he stares at the old willow tree once more before they continue their walk back to the cottage. Without the early morning fog, it is now clearly visible a bit further up the hill.

Kra makes a short crowing sound and flies up towards the cottage. Bo playfully follows beneath the rook, running between the stones and bushes over the grass.

Meanwhile, AnZhiMu, who is disguised in a brown cape to avoid the sinister spying man, is now returning home.
She rapidly walks towards the path, leading to the cottage. Cautiously she looks around and tries not to be seen as she hastily walks in the shadows of the trees and bushes along the sides of the path.
Back in the village the suspicious, sinister man has been waiting for quite a long time. Finally, he sees the other lady leaving the house on the opposite side of the street.
After that, the vendor comes out and continues working behind his stall.

The sinister man loses his temper and with a loud crack smashes his fist down on a wooden shelf in the stall he is still lurking in. The shop owner shrinks away in fear and tries to hide himself behind a few chests.
The baskets on the wooden shelf tremble and some fruit rolls out over the shelf and finally drops on the ground.
The menacing figure grumbles furiously, wraps his cape around himself, walks across the street and stares right at the vendor, who continues to look through the items in his stall pretending nothing has happened. After some moments a grey horse and wagon with some vegetables comes down the street. The sinister man has to move aside but first he turns his head toward the approaching vehicle, then he turns his head to the other side and stares down the street. As the wagon comes closer, the driver starts yelling at the cloaked figure to move aside. Like a statue in the middle of the street, however, the cloaked man remains in his position.

The wagon driver now shouts angrily and anxiously starts pulling back on the reins he is holding in order to stop the horse and the wagon. When the vehicle comes to a stop, obviously annoyed, the driver stands up in his wagon, yells and raises his hand. But his complaints come to a sudden stop when the sinister man turns around towards him.
The horse neighs and seems eager to leave. The driver bows his head, silently sits down and just stares at the ground before his wagon. As the eerie man walks away, the driver hears his walking stick scratching the sandy street surface.
The malicious figure slowly returns towards the street he came from and seems to blend back into the hustle and bustle of the busy street.
The wagon driver looks at the vendor, who is taking a deep breath of relief. The vendor frowns and shakes his head a few times. He looks up rather worried but then flashes a tight, meaningful, smile. The driver slightly nods and instructs his horse to continue down the road.
As the vehicle moves along, the vendor looks at the shop on the other side of the street. He notices the shopkeeper is slowly recuperating and collecting the fallen fruit.

Luzette and Kanoa now arrive at the cottage. Bo, barking and jumping before the door, has apparently already awoken the mother dog because a lower-pitched barking can be heard coming from within the cottage.
Kra sits on top of the high barn roof, behind the cottage. The rook looks around, scouting the environment and watching the boy and girl as they approach the door.

As Luzette opens the door, she softly hushes the dog and hangs her shawl on the wall next to the door. Kanoa looks up toward the rook on the roof and questioningly bends his head a little askew to see if Kra wants to come inside.
Kra now jumps off the roof and flaps its wings a few times before landing on the shoulder of the boy. He starts to pet the bird, but when he steps into the cottage, Kra shrieks and turns in the opposite direction.
When Kanoa stands still in the doorway, Luzette looks over at him and can just barely hear the rook crow a few times very softly near Kanoa's ear before it flies out the door. Kra then loudly crows twice and flies straight up into the sky.

Much further north, underneath a cloudy sky, the hawk descends into the small forest in between steep, rocky hills. As the surrounding area is made up of wastelands and barren plains full of creepy rock formations, these few trees actually seem like a little oasis.
Hidden behind some trees and bushes, there is a large cave entrance in the steep stone hillside. In the open area in front of the bushes are the recent remains of a fire and various gnawed-off bones scattered around. These leftovers reveal that, somehow, there is life in this harsh environment.

While the hawk slowly descends in circles above the open area and the remains of the fire, it screeches loudly every now and then. When it finally lands in a dead tree nearby, it seems to watch the cave entrance. An eerie screech again cuts through the air as the hawk restlessly waits for something or someone.

Not long after this screech, the cave's entrance emits a sudden rumbling sound. After a short silence, various shuffling sounds fill the air and loud, slow and irregular footsteps can be heard coming from the cave entrance.
Low-pitched grumbling sounds become increasingly louder as if someone is walking out.

Stooping under the ceiling of the entrance and almost stumbling over a large bone, a seemingly half-asleep figure steps out, rubbing one of his eyes with a fist.
He is rather hairy all over his body, except for his balding head, and has an especially heavy and protruding brow. He is at least twice the size of a grown man. The giant's sparse clothing, consisting of just a few dirty rags and pieces of leather and fur, reveals his enormous proportions. He seems to have three bellies wobbling on top of each other.

When he removes his hand from his eye and looks around grumpily, he still seems somewhat confused.
The hawk flies up towards him and, while he squints his eyes, he stretches his arm out in order to have the hawk land on it.
The hawk screeches once more before it lands on the leather band around the forearm of this large and voluptuous creature.
When the giant notices the little scroll of parchment on the hawk's leg, he grumbles and curiously tries to fetch the piece of paper. The hawk is obviously annoyed by his clumsy behavior and shrieks while it raises its foot.
The giant grumbles once more and finally manages to remove the tiny document. As he tries to unroll it with his huge hands, the hawk flies off immediately, high over the trees, back towards the brighter southern sky.
Just then, a somewhat younger and less corpulent giant comes stumbling outside as well. Although he is still quite frightening, he is a bit smaller than the other.
As the elder giant unrolls the little document, he loudly calls for the younger one and gives him the little scroll. The smaller of the two briefly, but scrupulously, looks over the miniature paper and is obviously disturbed by the message.

He looks at the anxiously awaiting elder giant and starts mumbling. The elder one responds with a short, questioning yell. While the younger giant hands over the piece of parchment to the elder giant, he once more looks at the tiny document. Anxiously mumbling, the older giant grabs the paper, briefly looks at it and turns towards the mouth of the cave. He pushes aside the startled smaller giant, bends down and disappears into the cave.

While all kinds of rumbling sounds reverberate out of the cave, the younger giant curiously looks at the sky but the hawk has already faded into the hazy atmosphere. The sound of things being dropped, shuffled and moved around can still be heard coming from the cave's entrance. But suddenly the sounds stop. A short yell precedes the ominous pounding footsteps of the giant coming out of the cave.

Meanwhile, Luzette stirs the fire a little and sits down at the table next to Kanoa. Bo lies down close to the basket with the two other young dogs. They seem to be more curious now and no longer reject the little black dog.
The boy and girl quietly stare at the table, where Kanoa's hand rests, holding and slowly rotating the marble between his finger and thumb.
As AnZhiMu approaches the cottage, far to the south Zuberi is deliberating with the elders of the tribe. Keiji still leads the horsemen and carriage further down the mountainside toward the cottage while Baaqir slowly rides toward the mountains and castle in his fantastic, yet creaky, wagon-house. None of them is able to see the hawk, rapidly diving through the air, returning to the cloaked, sinister figure standing near the stone wall of the village in the east.
Luzette and Kanoa are still gazing at the marble as the elder giant wildly runs out to the open area, fanatically, and wildly waving a golden crown above his head. He incoherently screams a few times, stomps his foot and then takes a very long, deep breath before letting out a prolonged, terrifying, earthshaking scream that echoes towards the south.

5. History

While the early morning gradually develops into a bright autumn day, AnZhiMu returns and enters the cottage, where the boy and girl are still sitting around the table quietly staring at the marble.
The opening door causes them both to look up at the entrance a little startled. Kanoa closes the hand with the marble, stands up and puts it away in his pocket.
Luzette also rises and walks to the door where AnZhiMu now hangs her second, brown cloak on the wall.

Kanoa slowly walks to the dog's basket and squats down while he curiously keeps an eye on Luzette and AnZhiMu, who are whispering and gesturing somewhat nervously.
While Luzette holds her hand on the brown cloak, AnZhiMu is obviously explaining using gestures that she was being followed in the village earlier when she returned from visiting Baaqir.

Luzette walks to a chest and opens it. She bends down and after some searching she takes out a fairly large, old, flat and leather bag of some kind.
It contains various documents, stacked between the bottom part and decorated leather top piece. She closes the chest, walks to the table, and lays the heavy leather folder gently in the center of the table.
Then she sits down and questioningly looks at AnZhiMu.
AnZhiMu sighs and nods her head a few times while she moves towards Kanoa. As she walks over to him, he slowly stands up. The lady gestures for him to sit down at the table as well. A bit tense, he walks to the table and sits down beside Luzette. AnZhiMu follows him to the table and calmly sits down as well.

Luzette looks at AnZhiMu and the leather folder on the table in a nervous but excited way.
Kanoa wonders if it may shed some light on this morning's extraordinary events, and provide the explanations he is yearning for.
All the excitement about the marble and meeting all of these new people did not seem to bother the boy.
However, AnZhiMu can tell that his mind is restless and puzzled. She looks into his eyes and slowly opens the folder by pulling a thin, red cord.

As she slowly opens the thick, decorated leather cover, she reveals a collection of drawings on various sizes and colors of parchment. The drawings are similar to those in Baaqir's book but they are newer and more colorful.
Luzette's eyes widen as she looks at the images on the first piece of parchment, showing her eagerness to witness the story about to be revealed.

Kanoa recognizes elements of this first drawing. Luzette points at a character and says "Eadwin".
It looks like a young king, wearing a golden crown with a black marble. Kanoa immediately fetches his marble and holds it above the drawing. Luzette looks at Kanoa, at the marble and then at AnZhiMu. The lady looks at the marble and slowly stretches out her hand.
While nodding approvingly, she gently closes his hand.

The drawing shows that King Eadwin was married and surrounded by kind and loyal people.
In the drawing there is also a castle in the mountains, which looks just like the view to the west when Keiji left. Kanoa points at the castle and asks "Keiji?"
Luzette immediately nods and points toward the castle and repeats Keiji's name and mentions King Eadwin's name as well. Kanoa now comprehends Keiji's sudden departure; he went to the castle to inform King Eadwin about the marble.

AnZhiMu now turns to the next sheet of parchment.

It is a drawing of a majestic royal chamber in an eastern palace. A sultan is shown with his wife and a small child. The sultan's wife seems to be a young AnZhiMu.
Kanoa looks carefully at the portrait of this woman and then looks at AnZhiMu.

She softly sighs and looks down. Luzette now points at the woman and tenderly says AnZhiMu's name. She then points at the little boy and says "Keiji". As Kanoa looks closely, he smiles slightly as he recognizes little Keiji.
But Kanoa suddenly realizes that AnZhiMu seems to be pained by this image, which obviously reveals how different their lives had been. Apparently she and Keiji were part of a royal family in an eastern realm many years ago.

As Luzette now turns another page of parchment, AnZhiMu seems a little stirred by these memories and she moves her hands in front of her eyes to hide her emotions.
The next page shows an image of a tribal leader in a desert-like setting with a few small groups of tents very far away in the background. Closer by, there is a settlement with one large, round tent, numerous camels and horses around an oasis further back and, in the foreground, some evidently important elders or leaders.
Looking carefully, Kanoa sees two children in front of the man who is obviously the chief. One of them is plainly recognizable as Zuberi. He is as tall as the chief but bends down and holds the hand of the other child, who looks a bit younger and is probably his brother.

Beside the leader stands a man who resembles Baaqir and seems to be a village elder, a medicine-man or mage of some kind. Kanoa points to the figure and asks "Baaqir?"
Luzette nods and while she slowly turns to the next document, Kanoa seems to realize that Zuberi, AnZhiMu and her son Keiji all have royal blood.

As Luzette turns to the next document, she nervously lifts up the parchment to look beneath it.

AnZhiMu soothingly points at another document below that juts out of the pile on the table. Luzette sighs and carefully pulls out the obvious missing page and carefully lays it on top.
It is a peculiar and colorful drawing that seems to have been made by a child. The subjects are spread over the whole sheet of parchment.
Kanoa notices Luzette just staring at this picture. He suspects the drawing is hers, since it shows the cottage they are in now and a little Luzette, with long, dark-brown hair.
There is also a sun, a rainbow, some trees, and hand-in-hand with Luzette what appear to be her parents. He points at the girl in the drawing and looks at Luzette. A blink of her eyes and a brief, faint smile confirm his thoughts.

Now AnZhiMu turns to another page, containing various smaller drawings. Together they seem to tell a little story, so Kanoa looks at them carefully one by one.
When the boy focuses on the first small drawing, he knits his brows and moves his head closer to the document.
It shows a king, wearing a crown with the black marble, riding with the queen and some guards. They ride through lush farmlands, fields and forests.
The mountains in the background show they are going in a northern direction.

The next picture shows that the entourage is attacked by a group of five giants, who vary in age and in size.
While the guards try to protect the king, one of the oldest giants, grabs the crown and harshly knocks the queen off her horse, against a rock.
Kanoa squints his eyes to examine the next small drawing showing a funeral, a king without a queen or a crown, surrounded by many leaders from other lands.

The next drawing shows two groups preparing for a large battle. On one side there are the five giants, who seem to be a father, mother and three sons.

On the other side are tribal warriors on camels, led by Zuberi's father, from the south, several fighters from the east including the sultan, Keiji's father, and a young AnZhiMu, and in front of them, from the west, the young, crownless King Eadwin, surrounded by many knights and armed guards. These parties seem to have decided to fight the giants to get the crown back. There are also two figures added later by a child's hand. As they are so similar to the ones in Luzette's drawing on the previous page, Kanoa surmises they are the parents of Luzette, standing beside the sultan and AnZhiMu. For some reason, it seems Luzette's parents also participated in this battle alongside AnZhiMu and the sultan.

While his eyes slowly focus on the next little drawing, Kanoa's swallowing slightly disturbs the silence.
This picture shows a large battlefield. The female giant, standing in front of her three sons, is injured by several spears and killed by a big rock, cast from a stone-throwing device used by the king's guards.
One of the sons also lies on the ground dead. The red color of blood is spread all over the bottom half of this drawing.

The eldest giant lies on the ground severely injured and seems to be holding up the golden crown.
Kanoa can see that there is a hole in the crown where the marble should be. Amidst all the fighting, the black marble has apparently fallen out and vanished.
In the sky above the battle flies a black bird. In the space between the bird and the battle below there is only one black dot.

In the next little drawing the older giant is holding a bloody knife in his hand and has a terrifying expression on his face. The younger giant is still a child, who seems startled and afraid as he bends down over the sultan from the east, lying on the ground and covered in blood.
These two remaining brothers seem to be the only ones left of their kind.

Kanoa squints once again at this drawing and then sees more casualties close to the sultan's body.
The older giant is looking at a young AnZhiMu, who is lying on the ground, severely bleeding from her throat. King Eadwin sits on his knees and holds her head in his hands.
Zuberi's father, the tribal leader from the south, also lies on the ground and apparently did not survive this battle either.

Kanoa does not dare to look up since he now understands the suffering AnZhiMu had to endure. Although King Eadwin probably saved her life, she lost her husband and, with one cut of a giant's knife, her ability to speak as well.
As he is staring at the image, Kanoa once again sees the same two figures as were drawn on the previous page.
It seems Luzette's parents did not survive this terrible battle either, since they are both drawn lying on the ground in a pool of red blood.

Kanoa finds himself incapable of expressing his feelings. It is as though he can almost feel the grief of Luzette as a little child losing her parents. Filled with sorrow, the boy looks up and sees Luzette trying to suppress her grief by smiling slightly with a somewhat quivering lip.
Although these sketches have clarified a lot, the room is now filled with a quiet sadness.

As if Bo had sensed their unease, the little dog is awakened by this silence. It gives a little innocent howl followed by a sneeze, which makes things come back to life again.
The sneeze wakes up the other dogs and now both of them bark softly and yawn. The little black dog stands up, shakes itself and slowly walks to the table.
While it gently climbs up onto Kanoa's knees, the tense silence seems now somewhat broken and AnZhiMu gradually turns to the next page of parchment.
While Kanoa gently caresses Bo's head, he looks at the next page, which again contains a few smaller drawings. They show a gray, dark and somber setting.

There are smoldering forest fires as well as deserted and plundered villages in these pictures. It seems the lands were filled with chaos and misery after the battle.

One drawing shows a picture of a new ruler in the east. His face is rather stern and unfriendly.
Another drawing shows AnZhiMu, accompanied by her little son Keiji and the orphaned Luzette, recovering in the castle with the lonely King Eadwin.

The next drawing, obviously one from Luzette as a child, shows how AnZhiMu, Keiji and she come to live in the cottage together.

The next sketches show that Zuberi's younger brother, still a child, is accompanied by a man. This man was also portrayed between Zuberi's father and Baaqir in one of the previous pictures. Apparently, Zuberi's brother and his uncle have taken over the leadership of the southern tribe, as they are clearly drawn in front of the others in their settlement.
On the side of this last little sketch, Zuberi and his uncle Baaqir are shown leaving the settlement on two camels.

Luzette turns the page and the last piece of parchment is revealed. This last drawing shows Baaqir traveling to the village in the east. And, on the bottom part, one more little drawing by Luzette shows Zuberi coming to live with them in the barn behind the cottage. Luzette and Zuberi are shown happily holding each other's hands up high.
After all the sadness and misery Kanoa has seen in these images, this small, simple sketch, actually not much more than a few lines drawn by a little girl, many years ago, gives him some joy.

He takes a breath, holds it a while, as if he is about to say something, but then slowly sighs, letting all of the air out of his chest.

Kanoa nods his head vaguely a few times as he allows himself to comprehend the exceptionally sad history of these people.
He then fetches the marble out of his pocket and holds it before him. While he stares at it, his mind seems to be flooded with thoughts. Everyone he has met this morning lost someone in this battle long ago.
A battle for what? Just a crown and a marble? It is difficult for the boy to understand.

AnZhiMu and Luzette silently watch Kanoa put the shiny marble back in his pocket, gently stir Bo and guide the little dog to the ground.
He looks at both of them, slowly stands up and, while quietly sighing, walks to the window.
He remains wandering through his thoughts for a while as the innocent Bo joyfully walks around his feet.
While Luzette stares at the last drawing, AnZhiMu watches Kanoa silently gazing over the trees.

6. On the Way

Far beyond the trees Kanoa is staring at, Baaqir is slowly driving his carriage down the road toward the castle. When he sees the king's wagon and company approaching from the other direction, he gently guides his horse to the side of the road and, with some creaks and rattling, brings the whole wagon-house to a stop.
As he slowly climbs off the wagon, it is not certain whether the cracking sounds come from his aging body or the wagon-house.

He recognizes Keiji, who rides toward him in front of the others, and seems pleasantly surprised as he yells his name.
Keiji stops his horse, swiftly jumps off, and runs to Baaqir, who opens his arms. They embrace each other briefly but intensely and Baaqir's low-pitched laughter makes Keiji smile. He puts his old, weathered hands on Keiji's shoulders and takes a good look at him.

Meanwhile, King Eadwin's wagon has also come to a stop. One guard has already dismounted and is opening the door of the carriage to let King Eadwin step out.
Keiji turns around and when the king approaches, he gently bows his head and steps aside. Baaqir and Eadwin warmly shake hands and embrace each other. Baaqir makes some gestures and points at the castle. King Eadwin laughs, nods and waves as they both walk back to their carriages again.

Keiji continues leading the king's company along the path towards the cottage. King Eadwin waves out his window to Baaqir, who is already sitting on his driver's seat.
The old man smiles and waves back while he urges his horse to continue on the road toward the castle.

In the southern settlement, Zuberi and his younger brother come out of their meeting in the large tent and walk past the guards standing on both sides of the corridor. They are followed by their uncle.

All three seem to be preparing for a journey and some type of formal event as many camels are gathered and Zuberi's brother has a woman bring him his formal wardrobe. The garment is made of leather and decorated with colorful beadwork.

Zuberi lays one hand on his younger brother's shoulder and nods. He then looks at his uncle, the chief, and nods seemingly out of a sense of obligation.

Then he turns, swiftly walks to his camel and mumbles something to the animal. As he climbs onto the camel, it immediately rises and starts walking.

As soon as he gallops out of the settlement, Zuberi raises one hand in the air for a moment and rapidly heads back through the dunes.

Kanoa turns around and sees Luzette softly sweeping one finger over the sketch of Zuberi and her as a little girl. When she looks up, she quickly closes the folder, stands up and puts it back into the chest.

Kanoa bends down to cuddle Bo a little bit. As Luzette walks to the window, she bends down near Kanoa, softly pets the little dog's head, stands up again and stares out of the window for a while as well.

Suddenly, Luzette points outside and then exclaims "Eadwin, Keiji".

Realizing the king is coming, Kanoa stands up. He takes out the marble and looks at it for a moment before putting it away in his pocket again. A bit nervously, AnZhiMu also stands up and walks to the door.

Her eyes barely dry, Luzette runs outside to welcome back Keiji and, of course, greet the king and his companions.

Kanoa just briefly smiles as he watches Luzette's innocent ability to simply move on and grab the next joyful moment.

As AnZhiMu passes Kanoa, she stops and they look each other in the eyes for a moment. Then they hear Luzette's voice outside yelling Keiji's name, horses' whinnies and neighs and an approaching vehicle with wooden wheels rumbling over the path.
AnZhiMu carefully embraces Kanoa. The boy feels a bit confused, but not uncomfortable and his arms slowly return the embrace.
She then smiles, gently pats him on his back twice and takes a step back. While still holding his shoulders, she looks from his eyes to his toes and back. Then she gestures for him to step outside as well with a slight, seemingly proud, smile on her face.

Kanoa walks out the door and sees Keiji step off his horse. AnZhiMu's son briefly greets Luzette and then leads his horse to the trough behind the cottage.
The king's carriage travels very slowly over the last stretch of the narrowing path towards the cottage. As Luzette joyfully waves with one hand, the wagon stops and the men begin to dismount.

All the horses make Bo a little restless and the little dog barks a few times as it runs around Kanoa's feet.
Kanoa bends down and quietly calms the little black dog as AnZhiMu slowly and curiously comes walking out the cottage. One guard now opens the carriage door and King Eadwin carefully steps out.

When the king sees Luzette softly clapping her hands and joyfully smiling, his rather serious expression immediately transforms into a big smile. As he walks towards her, his laughter sounds kind and comforting. He gently lays his hand on Luzette's head as she bows before him. He then puts his hand on her shoulder and briefly looks at the young woman with a big, soothing smile.
While King Eadwin turns around, Kanoa hears AnZhiMu suddenly taking a deep breath and slowly stepping in the direction of the king.

King Eadwin seems to notice her nervousness because, all at once, his expression turns quite serious when he looks at AnZhiMu. Kanoa just stares at them.

As King Eadwin and AnZhiMu move closer, slowly at first but then with increasing speed, their hands reach out to the other. Just as Keiji is coming back from behind the cottage, he sees his mother and Eadwin approaching each other.
Knowing that his mother was silenced by the knife of an evil giant years ago, Keiji stops and is astounded to hear his mother make a humming sound while she embraces the king. Luzette immediately brings her hands over her mouth and all the others silently watch them. Kanoa seems to shiver for a moment and blinks his eyes a few times. But the boy keeps staring at AnZhiMu, who now just hums very softly as she and the king embrace in an intense, profound and heartfelt way.

The little dog softly moans, looks down and holds its tail between its legs. Kanoa bends down and softly cuddles Bo.
The king and AnZhiMu, obviously still quite affected by their reunion, now slowly walk to Keiji.
As they approach him, King Eadwin softly and briefly places his hand on the young man's shoulder.
While AnZhiMu recuperates, Kanoa realizes they are coming over to him and he nervously stands up.
He now feels all the people present are looking at him. He hears some soft sounds of the horses, the leaves crackling under slowly moving feet, and the crunching sand under the boots of the approaching king.

He suddenly feels AnZhiMu's hand against his arm and as he looks up, he sees the king standing before him.
Kanoa nervously bows his head and, all of a sudden, he grabs the marble out of his pocket.
He holds it out in his open hand, somewhat close to King Eadwin's face. He briefly looks up once more and then immediately looks down again.

The king is astonished by Kanoa's sudden action. But after a short silence and a moment of staring at the marble, the king utters Kanoa's name and bursts into joyous laughter.
He moves both his hands to the marble, still laughing, and gently closes Kanoa's hand containing the shiny marble.
For everyone, the tension immediately dissolves. Kanoa starts smiling and puts the marble back in his pocket.

Everyone relaxes and begins laughing. The knights and guards behind the king, who seemed very alert and watchful at first, now laugh the loudest.
Keiji simply smiles, and AnZhiMu, still somewhat emotional, finally smiles a little as she hears King Eadwin's laughter.
Luzette joyfully watches how the king looks at Kanoa and reaches out to grab both of his shoulders. Kanoa looks up at him a bit shyly as the king observes the boy from head to toe and back.
King Eadwin moves one hand to AnZhiMu's back, she puts one arm behind the king and her other arm around Kanoa. For a brief moment, Kanoa feels completely at ease as he is embraced by these two friendly people, whom he knows share such a sad history.

Gradually the guards start caring for their horses. AnZhiMu and the king walk to Keiji. The three are deliberating while repeatedly pointing to the east, beyond the village.
Apparently Keiji is being sent off to inform the ruler of the east about the discovery of the marble. Keiji, who has already travelled a lot today, has a dejected look on his face.

AnZhiMu briefly holds one hand against his cheek and, with an understanding smile, insists that he has to go. Keiji finally nods approvingly a few times and smiles. King Eadwin firmly lays his hand on Keiji's shoulder, looks him in the eyes, and then looks to the east once more.
Subsequently he turns to his castle up in the mountains in the west, nods and slaps Keiji on his shoulder once more.

Keiji turns around and walks to the horse. He softly whispers to the animal as he gently runs his hand through its mane and is satisfied to see an almost empty trough.
He swiftly mounts the horse and approaches the path. As he passes AnZhiMu, she holds up one open hand. She watches her son riding swiftly along the path toward the eastern palace beyond the village.

As Keiji disappears into the hazy eastern horizon, AnZhiMu gestures for the king and all his men to come into the cottage. King Eadwin looks at his companions and after some mumbling and whispering, he softly shakes his head and points toward the castle.
The others prepare for the journey back to the castle and they begin to turn the carriage back toward the path.
Then, all at once, Luzette walks into the cottage in a hurry.

AnZhiMu turns to Kanoa, looks at him, and then points at the castle up in the western mountains.
She grabs his hand and looks at him once more before she quickly walks into the cottage. It is clear that Kanoa will go with them to the castle in a little while.

As Kanoa stands there, watching the king and his men already preparing the horses and carriage, he feels a bit uncertain about what to do. He just stares toward the trees until he hears a shout coming out of the cottage.
Luzette steps out with a tray of mugs, some filled with tea, some with water and a few with milk. All the men now joyfully step towards Luzette, grab a mug and start drinking.
When Luzette looks at Kanoa, he briefly closes his eyes and gently shakes his head once. The girl smiles, puts the tray on a stump and returns to the cottage.
Kanoa slowly walks to the trees, sits down on a rock and stares into the sky. He then lowers his view and looks at the spot where Kra fell on the ground.
While taking a deep breath, he picks the marble out of his pocket and slowly turns it around between two fingers.

He stares at it for some time until King Eadwin approaches and gently puts his hand on the boy's shoulder.
The king sits down beside him. They both look at the marble a little until the suddenly louder mumbling of the king's guards attracts their attention. They turn to the guards to see them all looking at the door of the cottage.
As the king and Kanoa stand up and turn to the door, the sight of AnZhiMu and Luzette makes their mouths fall open.

The way AnZhiMu has draped various blue, semi-transparent shawls over her light-blue, silky robe looks astounding and Luzette's sparkling green blouse and long skirt shine brightly in the sunlight. They seem to be prepared for an official celebration.
King Eadwin now formally walks to AnZhiMu with a big smile on his face. He holds his bent arm before her and nods his head, as if he invites her to join him. With her head slightly tilted to one side and with a joyful smile, she lays one hand over the king's arm in order to proceed, gently and slowly, to the king's carriage.

The journey to the castle is about to commence it seems. All the guards and knights are preparing their horses. The driver opens the carriage door and bows while the king mounts the two stairs and enters the royal carriage.
When King Eadwin reaches out his hand and AnZhiMu carefully steps into the carriage, the guard bows again. Just before she disappears inside, she waves for Luzette and Kanoa to come into the carriage as well.

Kanoa stands still and smiles. His doubts about whether he should go straight to the carriage or to Luzette first make him feel somewhat uneasy.
As Luzette remains in the doorway and seems to look at him quite anxiously, Kanoa abruptly decides to step away in another direction. He goes over to where the guards had their break, and starts collecting a few empty mugs.
This brings a smile to the girl's face. She raises her eyebrows and brings one hand before her mouth.

She then rapidly walks towards Kanoa, fetches the tray and the remaining empty mugs and, still smiling, quickly walks back into the cottage.
When Kanoa follows her, he almost bumps into her in the door opening and a mug falls out of his hands. Just before it shatters on the doorstep, Luzette bends down and deftly snatches the mug out of the air. As she rises again, they look at each other for a moment. The girl grabs all the remaining mugs and places them on the table.
While Kanoa steps back, Luzette comes outside and closes the door.

The boy slowly turns towards the carriage, awaiting Luzette to accompany him to join the king and AnZhiMu.
As the girl starts walking toward Kanoa, she looks down the path, beyond the carriage and seems to see someone approaching. It is Zuberi, rapidly approaching on his camel.
Luzette shouts his name, waves one hand and starts running towards him, passing Kanoa and the carriage.
All the others look up, startled by Luzette's sudden yell.

One of the guards immediately draws his sword but King Eadwin looks outside and waves for him to stand down. The king obviously knows Zuberi.
The guards frown as they watch the tall, cloaked young man swing off his camel and remove his hood.
He is literally welcomed with open arms by a cheerful Luzette. Zuberi, however, sees the king stepping out of his carriage and greets the girl with a short smile while he commences towards the king with a quite serious look on his face.
As Zuberi nervously bows before the king, Eadwin gives him a warm, reassuring smile. The king seems to remark on how grown up he now finds Zuberi and does not seem bothered by the young man's strange physical appearance at all.
Kanoa sees them both look at the mountains in the west and he hears them mention Baaqir's name as King Eadwin points at his castle.

Zuberi nods a few times, looks into the carriage and kindly waves to AnZhiMu before he walks back to his camel.
He lays one hand on it, bows towards Kanoa, briefly smiles at Luzette and mounts his golden-colored camel.
As the camel rises, Kanoa puts up his hand to wave and starts walking towards the carriage.
Zuberi gently rides the camel down the path and King Eadwin returns to his carriage. Luzette now also steps into the carriage.
The guards all mount their horses and the restless neighing and whinnying of these strong, yet graceful animals urges Kanoa not to linger.

As Kanoa puts one foot in the carriage, Bo barks at him. Kanoa happily sees the king nodding and the boy helps the little dog jump up the steps and into the carriage.
Kanoa turns his head once more to look at the trees, the stream and the cottage. Perhaps he hopes to catch a glimpse of his little, blue-eyed friend, Kra. Kanoa steps into the carriage and, before he even sits down, King Eadwin closes the carriage door and initiates the departure by tapping twice on the wooden side of the driver's seat behind him.
Slowly and with creaking wheels, amidst the sounds of tapping hoofs and neighing horses, they all leave, preceded and followed by guards on horses. The carriage, pulled by two white horses, starts its journey back to the castle.

Zuberi is already way ahead of them since his camel travels light and fast. In the distance, halfway between himself and the castle, he can distinguish the house on the wagon.
Since he knows this must be his friendly uncle, Baaqir, he enthusiastically encourages the camel to quicken its pace.

Keiji, who travelled hastily on the dusty road alongside the village, now approaches the sultan's castle in the east.
The castle is situated in front of majestic, eastern mountains.
The trail of dust, created by his rapid voyage, draws the attention of the sinister cloaked figure, who is still spying around the village walls.

His hawk sits on his shoulder. The bird's eyes seem to be meticulously surveying the environment. The sinister figure now moves to a spot where he can view Keiji on his way to the east. The dusty trail reveals Keiji is heading towards the palace.

As he approaches the palace grounds and reduces his speed, he closes in on one of the four impressive watchtowers, which are connected by large walls. He rides through a large open gate and into a big stone courtyard. He does not see any people or animals, except for the guards and their horses.
All the guards are cloaked with their faces obscured so that they look eerily the same. Keiji silently rides on toward the impressive domed palace at the end of the courtyard.
His approach was seen from the watch towers and the sultan is obviously expecting him. The sultan stands, in formal attire, on the landing of a wide stone staircase in front of the palace, surrounded by a few guards.

Keiji seems quite comfortable in this impressive setting, and he calmly steps off his horse, looks up the stairs and bows. When the sultan waves for him to approach, the young man humbly starts walking up the staircase.

Keiji apparently informs the sultan about the recovered marble and the gathering at the castle in the mountains to the west.
He points towards the castle to the west and looks at the sultan, who maintains his serious expression and does not respond immediately. After some silent moments, he clearly decides that he must attend this gathering and commands a few guards to prepare the horses.
Keiji turns his head and takes his first step backwards down the staircase. He then slowly turns around and returns to his horse at a more rapid pace.
While he waits and watches the guards assist the sultan onto his horse, Keiji softly runs his hand over his horse's back and then jumps into the saddle.

When his three guards are also ready on their horses, the sultan gives some commands and immediately two guards, somewhat aggressively, spur their horses and gallop away from the palace. They are closely followed by the sultan, Keiji and the third guard.

Their path is not alongside the village but straight toward the castle it seems, since they charge over the dry fields creating a clearly visible trail in the direction of the lower hills and forests in front of the mountains to the west.

7. Gathering

The creepy, sinister character observes the dusty trail of the sultan, Keiji and the guards from his position on the village wall and once more prepares a little scroll of paper.
He attaches it to the hawk's leg before he swings his arm and releases the bird into the sky. It flies off to the north again, where threatening clouds hang above the far snowy mountains. It will not be long before the first signs of winter reach the lands.

At the feet of these mountains, between some eerie rock formations, the giants are running through the wastelands. Their steps are heavy and thunderous. A few resident black crows fly out of a dead tree, screeching as they see these two colossal characters pass. The older and larger colossus leads his younger brother. They are heading southwest. The younger one cannot keep up and rests for a moment while he leans on a rock. He bends down a little and breathes loudly a few times.
When he hears his brother yell, he stops, leans over to catch his breath and then looks up. He sees that his brother has stopped to take a break and is now beginning to drink noisily from a leather sack.

As the younger giant looks up at the sky, he sees the hawk approaching. He immediately yells to his brother and points a finger at the bird in the sky.
The older brother continues guzzling from the leather sack while he turns around. The hawk has apparently swooped down quickly and now flies just over him.
The giant swallows, chokes and coughs, and subsequently turns back to his brother to see the hawk land on the stones his brother was leaning on.

Agitated and still coughing, he walks to his younger brother and yells at him a few times, reaching out for the hawk. The hawk screeches and jumps further up the rock.
The younger brother holds up his hand and turns to the hawk slowly. It seems the hawk prefers him over his rough and careless older brother, as it quickly hops onto the smaller giant's hand.
The younger giant cautiously unties the tiny scroll of paper from its leg. As soon as he is finished the hawk hops two times, spreads its wings and flies back toward where it came from.

The bigger giant impatiently grumbles as his brother unrolls the paper. He looks at it, frowns and looks up at his older brother. The younger brother now points to the southeast, mumbles something and turns his pointing arm towards the south-west, where in the distant haze the green forests and mountains can faintly be seen.
The older giant loudly roars. He packs up his stuff, pulls up his belt containing a knife, a big sword and an enormous rolled-up whip, and starts walking towards the greenish, faraway lands. As soon as his brother starts following him, the bigger giant begins to run and his feet pound the earth at an increasing tempo. Since the younger giant has to carry several bags on his back, he is barely able to keep up with his brother.

In the west, the royal carriage rides between the mountains and is well on its way to the castle. Kanoa looks out of the open window, over the hills and mountains at the trees. He sees some small farms and a few houses. The few people on the roadside look up at the carriage as it passes. The boy hopes to see his little rook and muses over this morning's events.
Suddenly, Luzette shouts and points out the window. Both King Eadwin and AnZhiMu smile. When Kanoa leans to Luzette's side and looks out the window next to the king, he can clearly see the castle on top of the mountain they are approaching.

It will not be long before they reach the castle and Luzette is excited. Kanoa smiles and feels the marble in his pocket while he sits back and looks out of the window again.

Moments later, the road curves and the boy sees the back of Baaqir's wagon-house. He takes a breath and raises his hand, as if he is about to say something, but then the carriage driver yells and makes the horses stop.
With his head outside the window, King Eadwin investigates why they have stopped. When he sees the wagon, he smiles sits back down and simply says, "Baaqir".

Luzette opens the door at once and steps out of the carriage. This wakes up Bo who had fallen asleep under Kanoa's seat. Through the window Kanoa can see Luzette walking alongside the white horses and guards. Then she stops, exclaims "Zuberi!", and runs over to the wagon.

Kanoa decides to go outside as well. He looks at the king and AnZhiMu before he rises, bows a little and slowly steps out.
The black dog stretches and then carefully steps out of the carriage to follow Kanoa. Once outside, Kanoa first stretches his legs a few times before he proceeds to the wondrous wagon-house.
Luzette has obviously seen this wagon before because she runs straight to Zuberi, who is busy attaching his camel to the wagon alongside the strong, brown horse. Climbing the last, steep road up the mountain toward the castle with the high and heavy load of the wagon-house is too difficult for one horse to accomplish.
As Baaqir walks out from behind the vehicle, he notices how impressed Kanoa is by the magnificent little house on the wagon.
The old man smiles kindly at the boy while he pats Kanoa's shoulder a few times. Then he looks past the boy and starts walking toward the king's carriage. When he passes the guards and horses he briefly and softly touches the animals' backs.

King Eadwin, followed by AnZhiMu, steps out of the carriage and turns to Baaqir. As King Eadwin and Baaqir step towards each other, both men stretch a bit and smile.

But their meeting is suddenly disrupted by a guard, firmly saying King Eadwin's name.
When the king looks up, the guard points at Baaqir's wagon and subsequently at the royal carriage. He then draws a curve through the air showing the carriage passing the wagon alongside the road.
Since the roadside is rocky and uneven, only an empty carriage can safely pass the impressive wagon. Therefore King Eadwin and AnZhiMu stand back a little while Baaqir briefly looks at them once more and starts walking back to his wagon.

Zuberi runs his hand over the camel's back in front of the wagon-house while Luzette walks towards Kanoa and leads him a bit further back. The little black dog is sniffing the roadside behind Kanoa.

The guards urge their horses forward and they slowly pass the wagon. Then the royal carriage driver instructs the white horses to start pulling.
While he yells several commands and moves the reins regularly, the horses and the carriage finally slowly pass the wagon. But then the carriage suddenly stops because one wheel is stuck behind a stone.
The driver now stands up and makes even more noise until both the ropes and the carriage groan.
The carriage leans towards a deep gully. Two guards step off their horses, walk behind the carriage and start pushing. The carriage driver encourages the horses once more and, while the ropes and wheels groan even louder, Zuberi suddenly runs over to them.

His large appearance and the resolute way he holds his hand out in front of the horses make all efforts to move the carriage over the stone instantly come to a stop.

As the guards move aside, Zuberi starts pulling the carriage backward. The guards look at each other.

King Eadwin waves for them to assist Zuberi and they all start pulling the carriage back while the horses in front of the carriage restlessly stamp their hoofs.

Once the carriage has been pulled back a little, Zuberi stands back and waves for the driver to proceed forward again.

The driver encourages the horses to pull the carriage forward, while Zuberi and the two guards push and guide the carriage, so that its wheel just moves past the stone.

Luzette sees that the royal carriage is now able to continue and she softly, but joyfully, claps her hands.

The carriage comes to a stop just past Baaqir's wagon-house. The guards return to their horses and King Eadwin and AnZhiMu walk towards the royal carriage to step in.

As they pass Baaqir, sitting on the driver's seat of the wagon, they briefly wave at each other. Luzette walks over to the carriage and also waves at Zuberi, who is just climbing into the wagon's driver's seat, next to his uncle, Baaqir.

Kanoa approaches the royal carriage as well. He calls for Bo and the little dog comes running to him right away. The boy pets the animal's back when it steps into the carriage again.

Just before he steps in, he briefly holds out his hand towards the wagon-house, where the uncle and his nephew both nod their heads and wave back at him.

As soon as Kanoa sits down next to Luzette, the king closes the carriage door and instructs the driver to continue on.

With the sound of neighing horses, hoofs on the road and some creaky noises of the wooden wheels beneath the carriage, they all continue their voyage, up the mountain, to the king's castle.

After the last royal guard has passed, Baaqir's wagon starts moving as well. Although it is a very heavy load, together the horse and the camel manage to get the wheels turning.

It is quite a peculiar view, to see this magnificent little wagon-house being dragged uphill by camel and a horse with a gold-colored mane.
As they see the royal carriage disappear behind the next bend in the curvy road up the mountain, Baaqir and Zuberi continue their journey toward the castle as well.
They travel much slower than the royal carriage, however, because the two-storey house on the wagon seems to be somewhat unstable as they ascend the winding path.

Keiji, the sultan and his guards are traveling quickly from the east. Just like Keiji's horse, the other horses are swift and sure-footed. Their slim, muscled bodies slightly shimmer every now and then when the sun shines through the trees and bushes.

Far beyond those trees, back in the direction of the village in the east, Kra sits high up in a tree, hidden by the foliage.
The rook watches the hawk return from the north and land somewhere near the village wall.
The little, blue-eyed, black rook hops and turns around to see the castle far off in the mountains to the west. It bends down, spreads its wings and flies off the branch, out of the tree. Kra glides over the ground for a while and then curves through the air to fly off to the north.
The clouds to the north not only seem to hold the promise of the winter to come, but now also announce the two threatening giants drawing nearer.

When the royal carriage is close to the castle, at the last crossing with the path to the south, the southern tribal leaders can be seen approaching. Riding on camels, Zuberi's younger brother, his uncle and several formally dressed representatives climb up the steep path in a long caravan.
As soon as King Eadwin's company notices the southern leaders, he orders the driver to stop the carriage.
While King Eadwin steps out of the carriage, Zuberi's brother instructs his camel to bend down and, while the camel does so, the boy steps off.

He walks, smiling gently, towards the king. His uncle follows him on his camel. The man seems to lack the ability to smile and his expression remains somewhat severe and unkind.

The boy bows before the king. King Eadwin lays his hand on the boy's shoulder and smiles. The young tribal leader looks up at his uncle, who looks down at them from up on his camel.

When the king also turns his head to him, the uncle just firmly nods once. King Eadwin points behind his carriage and mentions both Zuberi's and Baaqir's name to indicate they are approaching as well.

This pleases Zuberi's young brother and he questioningly looks at his uncle, who just frowns and, barely noticeably shakes his head once.

This response of his somewhat intimidating uncle makes the boy's smile disappear. When the boy turns to the king, he sees him gently smile and then pout briefly while he closes his eyes for a moment.

The young leader smiles again and yells some things at the other camel drivers with a certain determination in his voice. Immediately, all the camels start kneeling down and enable the men to dismount.

It is obvious they are eager to take a break since they all start to stretch their legs, fetch their drinking bags from the saddles and, somewhat loudly, celebrate their ability to finally rest. It is clear that Zuberi's brother has decided to wait there for Zuberi and Baaqir. The surly uncle is obviously rather displeased and growls before he harshly commands his camel to walk over to the others.

There he steps off, walks to the side of the road, leans on a rock and looks at the castle up the mountain, not so far away.

With a smile, King Eadwin slaps the boy's shoulder and enters the carriage again. He closes the door and the whole royal parade proceeds to the castle while the southern company, led by Zuberi's brother, waits for Baaqir and Zuberi to arrive.

The carriage passes the gate, enters the castle grounds and heads towards the courtyard.

The parade draws the attention of all the people around. Only the sounds of the animals can be heard as the carriage stops in front of the main entrance. The people quietly wait for the carriage door to open. Kanoa looks out the window and sees many noblemen, officially dressed figures, men, women and children in front of the impressive stone castle.

Luzette is clearly very excited and cannot wait to step out of the carriage. She moves her hand to the doorknob but AnZhiMu quickly stretches out her arm, lays her hand on the girl's knee and gently shakes her head once.

The king smiles and Luzette sits back silently. Two guards formally walk to the royal carriage door in a synchronized pace. One stands up straight while the other opens the door to allow King Eadwin to step out.

He is evidently pleased to see so many people gathered. When Luzette wants to step out next, once again, AnZhiMu stops her while she looks at Kanoa with a gentle, calming smile. The boy looks through the door opening and sees that King Eadwin is nodding and waving for him to come out.

Hesitating a bit, he rises, bends down and slowly steps out of the carriage. He hears whispering sounds all around the courtyard while he steps over to King Eadwin, who puts his hand on the boy's shoulder.

The little dog immediately jumps out the door and quietly, but restlessly, follows Kanoa. Then, AnZhiMu and Luzette also step out.

Escorted by guards, they all slowly walk toward the entrance, where two trumpeters simultaneously blow two short, low-pitched tones and conclude with one long, high-pitched tone.

When the trumpets are silenced, two guards turn toward each other, each grabs a large doorknob and simultaneously they pull open two huge, elaborately carved, wooden doors.

In the open doorway there is a friendly, smiling minstrel dressed in a greenish suit. He plays a few soft notes while he bows deeply and turns towards the big hall inside. As he invites them in, King Eadwin starts mounting the few stairs and gestures for Kanoa to join him.

As they slowly proceed toward the huge entrance step by step, a crowd of people gradually move towards them.
The guards keep a cordon around the carriage and allow AnZhiMu and Luzette to follow the king and Kanoa up the stairs.

Just when King Eadwin turns and guides the boy through the doorway with his hand, a buzzing and then an increasingly louder whisper can be heard coming from the gate. People start moving aside and seem to be startled or upset.
As almost everyone is now looking in the direction of the gate, the minstrel stops playing and both Kanoa and the king turn around to watch what is happening at the gate.

As Kanoa and the king are standing high on the steps and are able to look over the crowd, they can see Keiji, the sultan from the east and his guards enter through the gate and rapidly come riding towards them. They finally come to a stop behind the carriage.

The castle guards are very alarmed and gather around them. Keiji dismounts and is allowed to pass. He confidently walks to AnZhiMu, his mother, standing halfway up the staircase in front of the entrance.
He bows before King Eadwin, who slowly descends the stairs to walk to his new guests from the east.

The royal guards stay back now and allow the eastern guards to step off their horses as well. One of them assists the sultan as he also dismounts.
Both the king and the sultan look very serious. While a few horse sounds can be heard, everyone quietly watches them.

The king gradually smiles and reaches out a hand, which he gently turns to the stairs in order to invite the sultan into his castle. As King Eadwin returns to the entrance, followed by the sultan and his guards, the minstrel softly continues playing a few gentle notes and the crowd progressively starts mumbling and whispering.

While King Eadwin guides Kanoa inside the castle once more, the minstrel bows deeply and slowly follows them inside. The boy is relentlessly followed by the energetic, tail-wagging little dog. AnZhiMu is joined by Keiji and an excited Luzette. Together, they slowly enter the majestic hall.

8. The Hall

When Luzette hears the soft tones of the minstrel's instrument echoing through the grand hall, she almost starts dancing around, but her enthusiasm is tempered by AnZhiMu, who gestures for her to behave appropriately in this impressive environment.
In the center of the hall are two marble stands each topped with a red pillow. The marble stands are cordoned off with red velvet sashes.
Kanoa sees long, draped, colorful curtains hanging on the sides of the hall and also notices paintings and various shields, hanging high on the stone walls.
The boy stretches his neck and watches how the sultan, surrounded by his guards, proceeds into the hall.

When the boy turns around, the minstrel bows his head to him and slowly starts walking backwards over the stone floor towards the other side of the hall, where a marble platform holds an enormous, meticulously carved wooden throne with embroidered, red velvet pillows.
The throne stands between two large wooden chairs. As the dog seems intrigued by the minstrel, it begins to follow him, looking back at Kanoa.
The friendly smile of the minstrel draws Bo to the side of the marble plateau. Here, the minstrel takes one of the pillows off a chair, puts it on the floor and encourages the little dog to sit. Obligingly, Bo sits down on the pillow.

Kanoa looks around. He sees the king standing among several knights. He notices Keiji and, especially, Luzette admiring the hall's high, colorful windows. The boy then watches AnZhiMu, who seems a bit tense, looking around as well.

Seeing her dressed more formally within these majestic surroundings seems to emphasize the lady's mysteriousness for Kanoa.

As the boy decides to sit down on the edge of the marble platform, close to the little dog, AnZhiMu turns around, looks at him and smiles in a somewhat subdued manner.

The boy turns to sit down and is slightly startled to see the minstrel has vanished. After a short frown, he sits down on the platform. While he moves around a little in order to comfortably sit, his attention is drawn to the sounds coming from outside.

When the people around the entrance also start making more noise, Kanoa stands up again and sees King Eadwin hastily walk to the big, open doors. The sultan and his guards also seem to be exceedingly agitated.

A particular noise coming from outside grabs Luzette's attention. She suddenly shouts "Zuberi!" and rushes to the entrance. Luzette briefly bows her head to almost everybody she passes on her way outside.

Kanoa realizes that she must have recognized the sound of the camel and that Baaqir, Zuberi, and the wagon-house have probably reached the castle.

Kanoa is obviously relieved and decides to sit down again and just watch all the commotion from a distance.

He notices that Keiji seems to have found an acquaintance among the eastern guards. The minstrel appears near the door and is about to welcome Baaqir and his nephew.

Meanwhile, AnZhiMu moves towards Kanoa, staring at the center of the hall. When she lays one hand on his shoulder the boy startles in a way that makes Bo stand up and bark a few times.

Kanoa bends down and gently hushes the dog while softly stroking its black fur a few times. When he lifts his head again, he sees AnZhiMu looking at the big entrance door with concern.

As he stands up, Kanoa hears the crowd around the big door whispering and becoming increasingly restless.
Kanoa's eyes grow large as he observes the entrance of an impressive parade of southern leaders, among whom are Baaqir and Zuberi. The newcomers are closely watched by the sultan and his men.

King Eadwin gestures to a few guards and it seems the formal celebration is about to commence.
All attendees are carefully guided to the sides of the hall in order to free the center and the way to the throne, where King Eadwin now arrives and slowly sits down while he watches the two pillows on the stands, exactly in the center of the hall.
The king gestures for Kanoa to sit in the impressive wooden chair next to his throne. AnZhiMu follows Kanoa and stands behind the boy, close to the king's throne.
Keiji and Luzette take their place on the platform as well and stand next to the boy and AnZhiMu.

Kanoa feels it is almost time to hand over the marble and fetches the little, black, shiny ball out of his pocket.
He stands up and reaches his open hand out, offering the marble to the king.
AnZhiMu looks somewhat startled by this, while King Eadwin smilingly shakes his head. The king then looks at Kanoa and briefly holds one finger over his lips. He nods once while he gently closes the boy's hand.
Kanoa smiles a bit shyly, puts the marble back in his pocket and sits back down again. When he briefly looks at AnZhiMu, standing behind him, he sees how she is nervously looking around at the other guests.

In attendance are richly dressed noblemen and noblewomen, the sultan and his guards from the east, the king's knights, and the impressive southern delegation. There are also dozens of servants and guards all around the hall.
Gradually, the room falls silent. The minstrel begins to play a few soft tones and the king stands up.

With one hand held up, he waves to a guard standing next to a small door on one side of the hall and subsequently waves to another guard standing by a door on the other side.
They promptly open the doors and a procession of servants streams out of the doors on both sides. First, they rapidly assemble a long, light wooden table and place it between the wide entry and the two stands in the center.
Another group of servants lays white sheets over the table. As they rapidly leave, other servants start bringing in large trays of food, baskets with breads, fruit and several plates with steaming meat.
The last group of servants brings numerous cups and jugs and places them all on the large, now completely filled, table. Then most of the servants silently leave.

Kanoa looks at the table and seems very impressed. He also realizes all at once that he is rather hungry. He takes a deep breath and feels his belly. Then Kanoa notices the silence, which is suddenly disturbed by a cough from the king.

When the boy looks up, he sees the king staring at him in a friendly way. He sits up straight and looks around to find that everybody is watching him closely.
Suddenly the minstrel appears near the center of the hall and walks, slightly dancing, towards the boy while he softly plays a few notes.
The acoustic echoing within the otherwise silent hall gives the music a dream-like quality. As the minstrel stops before the boy, the echoes of his musical notes gradually fade into silence.

The king stands up and looks at Kanoa. As soon as the boy rises, King Eadwin waves once at the two trumpeters, standing in the enormous doorway.
They blow their tune again. It sounds much grander in this immense hall than it did earlier outside. The king steps forward and gestures for Kanoa to accompany him to the center of the hall.

Not exactly knowing how to express himself, either with a smile or formally and serious, the boy relaxes as he sees the soothing smile of AnZhiMu when he looks back over his shoulder.
He also catches a glimpse of Luzette, cheerfully, and Keiji, carefully, watching the entire scene.

When King Eadwin and the boy are halfway towards the two red pillows, the king waves to two servants, who quickly remove the poles and the red velvet sashes around the marble stands.
While the King and Kanoa slowly approach the two marble stands with empty pillows on them, a servant, holding a pillow with a silver crown before him, quickly but steadily walks to the center of the hall.
He stops and bends down a bit, while holding up the pillow with the silver crown on it. As King Eadwin stops, he carefully lifts the crown with both hands and cautiously places it onto one of the empty red pillows.

While the servant leaves, the king looks at Kanoa and the empty pillow. The boy understands that now is the time, and grabs the marble out of his pocket.

A short wave of soft whispering fills the air for a moment when Kanoa lays the black, shiny marble in the center of the empty red pillow on the marble stand.
He smiles as he remembers his first moments with Kra, the little rook. And, as if he is dreaming it, he hears a crowing sound somewhere above him. When he looks up with a slight smile, as if he is just following his fantasy, the crowd begins to stir.
Kanoa hears another crowing sound and looks up into the hall. Filled with curiosity he turns his head toward a small, open window high up near the ceiling, where the young black rook has obviously managed to get in.
Kra seems rather agitated. When the rook hops off the edge of the window and soars over the crowd, many startled shouts echo across the hall.

The boy realizes that it really is Kra and he joyfully smiles as he holds out his arm towards the approaching rook.
But, as the crowd becomes increasingly louder, the blue-eyed rook lands on the silver crown, causing it to wobble for a moment.
Kra crows a few times loudly and then hops onto the other pillow. As Kra lands on the pillow, the marble jumps up and bounces back on the pillow once before it rolls off the side and then falls on the stone ground.
Kra's crowing is hardly noticeable anymore as the hall fills with worried and frightened exclamations.

As Kanoa bends down and tries to catch the black marble, he hears screaming coming from outside. Because his eyes are drawn to the entrance for just a moment, he only touches the marble, but does not catch it.
AnZhiMu moves her hands before her mouth and both Keiji and Luzette step off the plateau and start running to the center of the hall. Bo runs after them and restlessly barks.
The marble now bounces on the floor in the direction of the long table, filled with food and drinks.

The screams from outside have become louder and are now accompanied by swelling, pounding sounds.
All the attendees begin to panic and even some guards start drawing their swords.
Kra flies back to the small window near the ceiling while Kanoa quickly follows the marble, now rapidly rolling towards the table.
Luzette, followed by Keiji, runs very quickly towards the marble as well. King Eadwin worryingly looks at the minstrel, whose eyes widen upon witnessing the violence just outside.
When the king turns his head and looks out the large, open entrance, he sees a furious giant throwing the guards, who are trying to stop him, against the ground.
The people in the courtyard now scream loudly and run away as the evil giant plows a path towards the large doorway of the hall. Inside the panicked attendees flee in all directions away from the entrance.

While Kanoa bends down to fetch the marble, rolling just in front of the table, he is shaken by a terrifying roar.
The hall suddenly becomes darker. The large, open doorway, through which the southern sunlight fell, is now blocked by a colossal, grotesque and furious giant.
He is so large that he has to bend his head to fit under the doorway to enter the hall. The giant is almost three times the size of the boy.

Startled and scared, Kanoa misses the marble again and it rolls on under the table. Kra obviously notices this, dives down and glides straight toward the rolling marble.
Luzette, still focused at the rolling marble, collides with an eastern guard. Keiji quickly helps her up again while Bo barks and runs around them.
A bit confused, they see Kanoa stepping back as King Eadwin guides him further backwards, out of the center of the hall.

The colossus steps inside the hall causing an eruption of frightened screams. He notices Kra skim over the floor and land under the table.
When he sees the little black rook hopping out from under the table with the marble in its beak, the evil giant utters a horrifying growl. He stomps his foot onto the white table, which instantly crumbles, launching bits of wood, white sheets, pottery, and all kinds of food across the hall.

While the giant, roaring loudly, approaches amid the deafening sounds of cracking wood, breaking pottery and shattering mugs and glasses, the rook shakes its feathers and barely manages to evade the falling chunks of food and fruit.

Kanoa loudly screams the bird's name. With the marble still in its beak, Kra flies upward, forcefully flapping its wings.
But its flight is violently disturbed by a swift, powerful punch from the right hand of the monstrously roaring giant.
Kra is knocked out of the air and flutters to the side while the impact propels the marble up towards the ceiling.

The rook's body and loosely flapping wings crash onto the ground and roll in front of Zuberi's younger brother, standing on the side of the hall. The marble is now floating through the air.

All at once the hall is silent. The giant's growl seems to reflect his vigilant stare, which follows the marble's path as it slowly descends to the ground.
Luzette, who also has kept her eyes on the marble, instantly runs to a chair. She jumps on it, bends her knees and leaps high above the floor, stretching out her arm and reaching for the descending marble.

The giant moves towards her, angrily stomping through the debris on the ground.
Just when Luzette grabs the shiny, black marble out of the air and prepares for her landing, the colossus reaches out to grab her.
Suddenly though, he steps on the shards of a big ceramic vase. He screams out in pain, retracts his arm and briefly looks at his foot. As Luzette lands on the ground, she sees the roaring giant quickly approaching and reaching for her. As she has no time to stand up, the girl immediately pulls back one arm, preparing to throw the marble to Zuberi who is standing nearby.

She swings her arm towards Zuberi with all her might but just before she is able to throw the marble, Luzette's whole body is violently dragged into the air by the rough, dirty hand of the furious giant.
He swings the girl around while tightly holding onto her hand, wrist and a part of her forearm.

As Luzette screams loudly, Zuberi immediately picks up his brother's decorated spear. He shouts furiously, runs towards the giant and plunges the spear into his foot.
The angry giant groans terribly and immediately turns to Zuberi, who quickly pulls the spear out of the giant's wounded foot and retreats.

Suddenly, Keiji comes running towards the giant. He jumps up into the air and drives his sword into the other enormous foot of the enraged giant holding Luzette. The tremendous pain caused by Keiji's sword makes the giant scream and turn his whole body.
The intensely and stridently screaming Luzette, who is still grasped in his wildly swinging hand, is flung against a stone pillar and is instantly silenced.

King Eadwin has witnessed this terrifying scene and, inspired by the courage of Zuberi and Keiji, he draws his sword and yelling as loudly as he possibly can, orders all of his guards to follow him and attack the colossus, who is still holding the girl with the marble in her hand.

As the king and all his men now step towards the evil giant, the colossal character angrily turns around, pushes aside some remains of the table with his foot, and walks towards the doorway.
He stomps through the mess, holding Luzette's limp and silent body in front of him.
The colossus stoops under the doorway and runs outside, where the younger giant, who now seems troubled by his older brother's violence, is still waiting in an empty courtyard with just a few horses and the king's heavily damaged carriage lying on its side.

Kanoa, Keiji and Zuberi run outside and, as they stand on the landing in front of the entrance, they only catch a glimpse of the terrible creature, followed by his smaller brother, running away with Luzette towards the north.

While Zuberi and Keiji stare at each other, Kanoa feels his pocket and remembers the marble, which must still be in Luzette's hand. He immediately turns back inside, where he sees Zuberi's brother and the minstrel bent over the little black rook on the floor. Bo restlessly walks around them with his tail down, softly howling every now and then.

9. Preparations

Kanoa slowly and carefully walks through the debris strewn over the floor, towards the minstrel, who cautiously slides his hand underneath the rook.
Then, while the bird's legs come out under his fingers, he gradually lifts up the bird. He supports its body in the palm of his one hand and holds its neck and back with his other hand while both wings of the rook hang loosely downwards.

Soft whispering and some mumbling can be heard, followed by a few crackles underneath the shoes of attendees, who are starting to move and look around, still perplexed by what has just happened. Most of the guards and knights slowly and silently sheath their swords and look at one another, still shaken and somewhat perplexed.
Many attendees fled for their lives during the giants' attack but some remained inside the hall, hiding on the sides and in the corners.
Some servants rush outside to help the guards, who are now standing up and brushing themselves off unsteadily. The guards who were tossed to the ground are carried into a building next to the castle. One of them looks dazed and has a bleeding hand but is already getting up.
It seems that, besides some bruises and scratches, nobody is severely injured.

As Kanoa proceeds to the minstrel, he is suddenly startled by a brief and subdued wailing sound. As he looks in the direction of the throne, the boy watches how AnZhiMu repeatedly shakes her head and leans against the chair Kanoa sat in earlier. AnZhiMu holds the chair tightly with one hand and, trying hard to suppress her emotions, holds her other hand trembling before her mouth.

She seems to gasp for air as she inconsolably grieves for her lost girl, who was so violently taken away moments ago.

When Zuberi and Keiji see the last contours of the giants disappear underneath the threatening northern sky, they seem aware that this is also the last they will see of Luzette.
They restlessly look at each other for a moment and catch their breath before they turn around and silently walk inside again. Keiji sees that the king and a few ladies have already gathered around AnZhiMu and are trying to comfort her, so he chooses to walk to the sultan's guards.
Zuberi's size and appearance automatically cause people to get out of his way. He walks to his brother, who is closely watching how the minstrel carefully holds the rook.
Kanoa bends down beside the minstrel and gently runs his finger through the neck feathers of the young bird, which keeps its eyes closed and does not move.

Gradually, the servants start to clean up the mess created by the short but intense raid of the malevolent giant.
AnZhiMu is escorted by a number of ladies to another room. As the noise level steadily rises, the groups of attendees seem to start reorganizing. King Eadwin is consulting his advisors. Similarly, all the southern guests gather around Zuberi's brother and his uncle. Keiji seems to be deliberating with one of the sultan's guards.

Meanwhile, from his vantage point, high on the old village wall, the sinister figure may have seen or heard some of the unrest at the castle to the west since he has been watching it closely. With the help of his walking stick, this sinister cloaked man now hastily descends the stairs and walks along the side of the street until he secretively enters a small, dark alley. After some moments, hoofs suddenly sound loudly on the stone road and a dark, whinnying horse, ridden by the sinister cloaked figure, emerges. While the echoing of the horse's hoofs makes people turn around, they all look away quickly as they notice the sinister cloaked man, who is heading off to the north.

The atmosphere in the hall slowly becomes a bit less tense. Servants begin setting up a table, less than half the size of the original table, and setting out the unspoiled food and drinks from the feast.
All of a sudden, some of the servants hear running sounds outside, rapidly approaching the entrance. Kanoa looks up towards the entry and he sees Baaqir, thin and bent with age, running back in from his wagon-house holding some small object in his hand.
As Zuberi sees his uncle coming towards them, he helps the minstrel, still holding Kra in his hands, carefully stand up.

Practically out of breath, Baaqir comes to a stop in front of them. With his empty hand, Baaqir caresses the bird very gently and quite noisily catches his breath for some time.
He then bends down a little and looks very closely at the rook's head. When he gradually rises again, he lifts his hands, revealing a tiny bottle. He cautiously takes off its tiny, rounded cap, which he holds under the black bird's beak for a while. His actions are closely watched by the minstrel, Kanoa, Zuberi and his brother.
The silence is almost audible until all at once, a soft crowing sound breaks the tension. Baaqir immediately takes the cap away and puts it on the little bottle before he carefully puts the flask in his pocket.

As the black rook weakly tries to move its wings, it stretches its legs and turns its head. Kra begins to open its eyes, first briefly and only halfway, but then fully.
They all smile and sigh with relief when they see the bright blue eyes of the little black rook.

Baaqir looks up at the window where the rook came from and then looks at the empty pillow on the stand in the center of the hall. He nods a few times as he surveys the mess and seems to realize that Kra had tried to warn them about the giant's approach earlier.

The minstrel notices the bird regaining its strength and, while gently holding one hand just above the rook, his other hand encourages the black bird to stand up on its feet.
Kanoa slowly reaches out his hand and watches how the black bird shakes itself, blinks a few times, stretches out and nods its head towards Kanoa.
With its wings still hanging somewhat loosely, it then hops onto the boy's hand and starts flapping its wings, which makes everyone smile and step back.
The minstrel is pleased with the recuperating rook as he gives the little bird a friendly smile and looks straight into its eyes for a moment.
With his hands now free, the minstrel steps towards Baaqir. They seem to know each other from before because they smile, open their arms and embrace like old friends.

Kanoa gently runs his fingers over Kra's neck and holds the bird just before him. Closing his eyes briefly, he carefully nuzzles the bird's head softly against his cheek.
He opens his eyes again and holds Kra before him once more. While he continues to caress the bird's neck, he starts looking around.

Most of the servants have left the hall. In the center, the silver crown still lays on the red pillow, a bit askew. Servants have just removed the other stand and pillow, which were meant for the marble. As a servant is about to pick up the silver crown, he first looks at King Eadwin for his approval. The king starts walking to the center of the hall, followed by his knights.
This catches everyone's attention and the hall grows quiet. The minstrel notices this and guides Kanoa, Zuberi and his brother to the center of the hall.

Kanoa wants to lift Kra onto his shoulder but the bird starts flapping its wings a few times. The boy understands that the rook wants to fly and he holds his hand up high, enabling the black bird to spread its wings and jump off his hand.

First the rook, still somewhat weak, seems to fall towards the ground, but Kra manages to skim over the floor, towards the center of the hall.

Then, really pushing its wings, it flies high up to the little window near the ceiling again, accompanied by many sounds of both alarm and joy uttered by the people below.

King Eadwin, proceeding to the center of the hall, seems obviously relieved to see Kra flying again as there is the shadow of a smile on his face when he stops before the crown, where the servant now bows.

As the minstrel escorts Kanoa, Zuberi and his brother toward the king, the sultan looks somewhat enviously at them and begins walking to the king as well.

He commands his guards to follow him and they march behind the sultan towards the king. Keiji, in his turn, walks behind the guards and proceeds to the center as well.

When Zuberi's uncle stiffly follows his nephews, Baaqir decides to humbly walk behind his brother and also proceeds towards the group of leaders in the center of the hall.

As the servant awaits the king's decision, Kanoa seems to realize that this crown has some deeper meaning to these people, just like the marble.

Looking up at the rook, now cleaning its feathers, high up on the window sill, Kanoa reaches into the pocket where he had kept the marble, but it is empty.

Frowning and a bit puzzled, he joins the circle around King Eadwin formed by the leaders from the west, the south and the east.

The minstrel walks around a bit and looks at the king for a brief moment. As the silence increases, everyone looks at the king, who picks up the silver crown and hands it to the servant, who gently takes it and bows before he walks away.

King Eadwin now picks up the pillow with one hand and throws it over the table, towards the big entrance and screams, releasing his aggravation.

The mumbling of the surrounding attendees suddenly gets louder when the king once more expresses his anger and disappointment by kicking the remaining marble stand to the ground.

With an apologetic grumble, King Eadwin looks around at the slightly startled group and walks to the table.
He picks up the red pillow he just threw and carefully lays it on an empty corner of the table. The king looks back at the others somewhat regretfully before he continues to walk outside.

This creates a more relaxed mood among all the guests, who are looking at each other a bit questioningly.
Kanoa, who is still a bit hungry, decides to follow the king. He walks to the table and fetches some bread and a piece of fruit. The little black dog has been sniffing around the table all this time. It now runs to Kanoa, who grabs a small piece of meat and presents it to Bo. While wagging its tail, the dog grabs the meat with its teeth and follows the boy, towards the entrance.

After they fetch some food and drinks from the table, Keiji and Zuberi now also head outside. Then, gradually, all the men start moving towards the table with the food and beverages.
Three groups gather around the table: the knights and castle guards, the sultan and his guards and Zuberi's family.
While the minstrel rearranges some plates, looks around and tries to be helpful, the three factions just watch each other while they consume their food.
Meanwhile, Kanoa stands outside next to King Eadwin. Both are staring at the dense, dark clouds to the north, under which the evil giants disappeared into the mist with Luzette and the marble.
The thickening fog underneath the clouds indicates that a snowstorm is approaching and just when they are joined by Keiji and Zuberi, the first snowflakes start swirling around in front of them.

Quite upset, Zuberi approaches the king, points to the north and says Luzette's name.
He then points at the horses and some of the guards, standing in the courtyard, and subsequently points to the north again. He clearly wants to leave for the north to find Luzette.

But the king just sighs. He follows a swirling snowflake, holds out his hand to capture it and slightly nods his head a few times. As the snowflake melts on his hand, Baaqir, Zuberi's brother and his other uncle, some knights and the sultan and three eastern guards all gradually come out onto to the landing.
Keiji joins the eastern guards and while the king turns to his other guests, Zuberi looks at Kanoa questioningly.
The boy's eyes immediately grow large. He feels quite honored but seems unsure about how to respond. He bends down and briefly pets the restless little dog. Then Kanoa stands up again, takes a deep breath, stretches his arm up and lays his hand on Zuberi's shoulder before he exhales nodding. Zuberi slightly bends down and puts his hand on the boy's shoulder for a moment. Zuberi smiles as he sees his younger brother walking towards him.

The younger brother is still closely followed by his uncle, who always tends to restrain him.
Zuberi understands that his brother will not or cannot come with him to the north and he tries to give him a calm smile when they embrace each other.
As Zuberi releases his brother, Baaqir steps toward his brave nephew and looks him in his eyes. Baaqir mumbles a few things, looks at the increasing snowfall, still gently blown by the northern wind, looks at Kanoa and sighs.
He turns his head back to Zuberi and puts his arm around his nephew's back. He nods and mumbles some things before he hastily walks towards his wagon-house.
Keiji is still standing near the sultan's guards, whose faces are obscured by their black garments.

Despite the fact that they all look identical, Keiji seems to have a particular interest in one of them. As they watch the northern clouds, the sultan approaches the king and points to the east, apparently determined to return to his palace very soon.

King Eadwin looks at the increasing snowfall and nods to show that he understands. The eastern guard and Keiji look at each other briefly before Keiji walks to Kanoa and Zuberi.

Keiji takes Zuberi's hands, firmly nods and mumbles some things while he turns his head to the east and then to the north. He looks at the eastern guard briefly and then looks back straight at Zuberi, who nods approvingly.

Keiji obviously intends to head to the east first for some reason.

Meanwhile, AnZhiMu has apparently recuperated a bit and stands in the large doorway. Bo runs to her and barks a few times. She bends down and gently pets the dog's head.

As she looks up she sees Keiji standing before her. She slowly stands up and as he puts his hands on her shoulders, he mentions Eadwin's name and gestures that she should stay in the castle for now.

Looking toward the north, he also mentions Zuberi's and Kanoa's names. Keiji then puts a hand on his chest and points eastwards before looking at the sultan.

AnZhiMu sighs and as she turns toward the sultan, he slowly walks over to her and briefly bows his head. She looks at the sultan while her hand guides her son to walk towards the eastern guards. The sultan clears his throat and grumbles a little as he sees Keiji walking towards his guards, but he utters no further sounds. He just politely nods to AnZhiMu, turns around and follows Keiji toward his guards.

With a short yell the sultan commands his guards to prepare for the journey back to the palace.

As they all walk to the stables on the side of the courtyard, Keiji looks back and holds his hand up high towards Zuberi and Kanoa before he disappears around the corner after the others.

As King Eadwin sees the minstrel staring off to the north, into the thickening clouds, he worryingly looks at Zuberi and Kanoa.

Meanwhile, Baaqir returns to the courtyard carrying a heavy sack. He stops at the bottom of the stairs, where he puts down the sack and looks up at his nephew and Kanoa. The boys look at each other and both start descending the stairs towards Baaqir, who slowly bends down and opens the sack.

When he looks up at the approaching boys, he suddenly looks behind them, toward the entrance to the hall, where he sees Kra flying out. The rook glides over the king and the others, flies up and, finally, while flapping its wings, lands on the stone banisters close by. The black bird shakes itself once and hops onto the end of the banister, where it quietly settles down.

Zuberi continues down the stairs to his uncle, who is still looking at Kra with a smile. Kanoa stretches out his arm and gently strokes Kra's neck feathers. He bends down his head and, with a smile, looks into its blue eyes. The rook turns its head a few times and softly crows.

Bo inquisitively follows Kanoa down the stairs. While the boy is still petting Kra, the little black dog sniffs around the stairway and restlessly walks out to the courtyard, where it runs a bit towards the north and starts barking loudly.

Kanoa stands upright, turns his head and watches how AnZhiMu quickly walks down the stairs towards the dog in the courtyard, bends down and tries to calm it by soothingly stroking the dog's head. She manages to guide the animal back to Kanoa, but Bo continues to look to the north regularly and restlessly make soft growling sounds.

When Kanoa squats down and reaches out his hand however, the little black dog approaches him and becomes less tense. Kanoa's hand softly pushes on the animal's back to make it sit down.

Bo sits but still softly howls every now and then while it looks to the north. The boy realizes that it may sense the giants' escape route as he stares in the direction in which Luzette was taken.

All of a sudden, the sound of several galloping horses draws everyone's attention. The sultan, his guards and Keiji have prepared their horses in the stables and are now commencing their journey back to the sultan's palace with great haste.
Keiji briefly waves to Zuberi, Kanoa and the others before they head back to the east. AnZhiMu holds up her hand as she sees them disappear beyond the trees, through the snowflakes, and into the forests.

The clouds now slowly slide in front of the sun, darkening the sky. The increasing snow and the thickening clouds emphasize the approach of the evening.
The day now progresses rapidly.

Zuberi's stern uncle is obviously eager to leave as well. He briefly nods at Zuberi before he walks to the king. He bids farewell to King Eadwin and walks down the stairs, where Zuberi stands up and nods his head towards his uncle, who proceeds to the courtyard and the camels.
When the younger brother of Zuberi intends to bow before the king, he is warmly embraced by King Eadwin.
While the southern tribal leaders follow Zuberi's uncle, the young leader from the south walks down the stairs to his brother.
They stand with their hands on each other's shoulders for a moment and they briefly, yet firmly, embrace one another before Zuberi's brother follows his uncle to the stables and camels.

King Eadwin walks to the entry and gives commands to two guards. One of them promptly walks into the hall and the other descends the stairs and runs towards the stables.
As the people from the south are leaving, AnZhiMu walks to Bo and gently squats down besides the little black dog.
In the meantime, Baaqir and Zuberi look at the items Baaqir is taking out of his sack. There is a long rope, a knife, several pieces of bread, a large cloth or tent and several other things.

All at once, the sound of neighing horses makes them all look up toward the courtyard. The guard, who ran to the stables, has returned with four men guiding four horses.
King Eadwin descends the stairs, motions for Kanoa and Zuberi to follow him and walks to these particularly fine and majestic horses. As he stands in front of the animals, he indicates that it is up to the boys to choose a horse.
Zuberi looks at Kanoa for a moment and walks straight towards a black horse. When the horse softly whinnies, Zuberi gently hums and runs his hand through its mane while he looks at Kanoa.
The boy seems unsure and walks towards King Eadwin. This causes Bo to get up, but AnZhiMu calmly makes the little dog sit down again, while she watches Kanoa and the king looking at the horses.

The king points at a light brown horse and looks at the boy questioningly. Kanoa however decides to step towards a dark brown horse with a black mane, which looks just like Keiji's horse. This choice seems to amuse the guards, since they have to suppress their laughter as Kanoa walks slowly, and somewhat insecurely, up to the athletic, dark brown horse. King Eadwin decides to escort him and helps the boy climb onto the restless horse.

Just when Kanoa tries to grab the reins, they are all startled by the yells of the southern leaders, urging their camels out of the stables and into the courtyard.
Kanoa's horse jumps up a little, scaring the guard and forcing the king to move back. Kanoa wraps his arms around the horse's neck to keep from falling while the horse restlessly gallops over the courtyard towards the camel caravan leaving for the south.
This view of the helpless boy on such a powerful horse makes even Baaqir laugh out loud for a moment.
As the horse approaches the camel caravan, Kanoa, with his head still halfway down the horse's neck, starts humming towards the ears of the noble animal.

Gradually, the horse slows its pace, allowing Kanoa to take hold of the reins. As the horse slowly turns, the camels continue south and Zuberi's brother smilingly waves one more time. Kanoa sits up and quickly waves his hand. Rather proud, he turns to the spectators and sees how Zuberi waves goodbye to his brother. Perhaps a bit too self-confident, Kanoa then briefly squeezes his knees.

Immediately, the horse neighs and lifts up its front feet, nearly causing Kanoa to fall backward. But he embraces the horse's neck once again and starts humming.

The horse calms down again and now marches steadily back toward the other horses, King Eadwin and Zuberi.

With a surprised smile on their faces, they watch the animal stop in front of them. Seemingly relaxed, Kanoa climbs off the royal horse. The boy hums a bit more while he gently runs his hand along the horse's dark-brown neck.

King Eadwin instructs the guards to return the remaining horses to the stable and puts his hand on Kanoa's shoulder.

When the boy turns his head, he sees the king nodding and subsequently turning to the entrance, where another guard, carrying two bags, comes running towards him.

The guard bows when he presents both bags to the king, who subsequently hands them over to Zuberi and Kanoa.

Zuberi looks inside the bag immediately and sees that it contains food, water, woolen gloves, a blanket and some other useful items for their journey to the north.

Baaqir walks over to his nephew with his sack, containing provisions, rope, a tent cloth and more, in his hands.

While Zuberi packs all of their things into the two bags with his uncle, Kanoa watches two female servants come walking outside with several capes, vests and cloaks.

10. The Journey

Kra has quietly been resting on the banisters. The little black rook even slept a bit. But now it sits up, shakes its feathers and crows. Kanoa looks up as he sees the bird flying towards him, and stretches out his arm. The rook lands on Kanoa's forearm but its flapping wings cause Kanoa's horse to stamp its feet and neigh restlessly.
The boy hums a few times and touches the horse with his other hand. This calms the animal down again and allows Kanoa to turn his head to the little black rook on his arm.

With one finger he strokes the bird's neck feathers and smiles. When the bird repeatedly steps up and down on his arm, the boy looks to the north. He looks at the clouds, the darkening sky, and the path he will soon follow with Zuberi in an effort to find Luzette and perhaps also the marble.
Kra looks at the boy's eyes for a moment, crows softly and then flies off his arm, over the courtyard, through the snowflakes, and into the sky towards the forests.

Meanwhile, Zuberi does not show much interest in the clothing he is offered. He just picks up a piece of leather armor and puts it around his chest. Then he lifts the bags and attaches them to his horse's saddle, one on each side.
Kanoa turns around and is not sure what clothing to choose. Since Zuberi wears a cloak and he left his own cape at the cottage, he chooses a nice warm greenish-brown cloak and hangs it over his shoulders.
While Kanoa tightens the front of his new cloak, AnZhiMu and Bo come walking towards him. Kanoa bends down and pets the little black dog. He feels a bit sad to leave his new little friend and, as if Bo senses his sorrow, the dog softly howls a few times.

AnZhiMu gently lays her hand on the boy's shoulder and, as he stands up, he looks her in the eyes, swallows, nods, and takes her hand with both his hands.

Zuberi has already mounted his horse and, while his uncle holds the horse, Zuberi looks at Kanoa. King Eadwin steps forward and assists Kanoa as he carefully mounts his horse.
Zuberi sees that Kanoa is not particularly experienced at riding a horse and he gently instructs his black horse to commence slowly.
He nods to Baaqir, AnZhiMu and King Eadwin. The king steps back and stands next to AnZhiMu. Kanoa leans down against his horse and starts humming again. He sits up and carefully squeezes his knees to have the horse follow Zuberi. The boy quickly turns his head and waves goodbye to Baaqir, King Eadwin, AnZhiMu and Bo.
Baaqir slightly frowns as he watches the boys leave. King Eadwin holds up one hand and sighs while AnZhiMu waves with one hand and holds the other in front of her mouth.
Zuberi and Kanoa slowly leave the courtyard and disappear through the trees and snow towards the darkening north.

Baaqir looks at the clouds gathering before the setting sun, fetches his sack and obviously prepares to leave in his wagon-house in order to be home before it gets dark.
However, King Eadwin holds up his hand and shakes his head, making it clear that he wants Baaqir to stay at the castle. Baaqir looks at AnZhiMu. She pouts a little when she nods a few times and closes her eyes for a brief moment.
The old man grumbles softly but he accepts that it would be unwise to travel down the mountain with his wagon-house in this weather and decides to follow them inside.

Kanoa follows Zuberi as they head north. The multiplying snowflakes still melt soon after they touch the ground.
The boy notices that there are no more farms or houses along their route. In the more open terrain they are heading for, the wind blows much harder and has already created small piles of snow.

The lowering sun paints parts of the clouds in the west a bright orange color, which contrasts with the remaining patches of blue sky in the south.
The dark clouds ahead of him make Kanoa tighten his clothing around his neck and he pulls the cloak over his head. Zuberi looks back, slows down a little and also pulls his cloak over his head.

When Kanoa's horse rides alongside his own, Zuberi smiles and matches the boy's speed and they continue side by side through the increasing snowfall. As the sun slowly sets, both riders then try to outpace each other repeatedly and finally gallop together at high speed. Before they know it, they are approaching the bare, white wastelands, riding swiftly over the last pieces of ground not yet entirely covered in snow.

As they pass the last trees they both slow down and look at the immense, seemingly infinite, parched land in front of them. There are only a few dead trees and irregular, and somewhat frightening, rock formations. Some are as small as a rooster and others are larger than a house. Ages of erosion have worn them into strange, eerie shapes. Some have holes that look like large, staring eyes.
Just before sunset, the grey clouds and thick fog begin to hide the snowy mountains in the distance. The wind in this eerie, open terrain lashes the snow against their faces. Once the sun has disappeared behind the mountains in the west, darkness seems to fall over them quickly.

While they gradually slow down and proceed over the white wastelands, Kanoa and Zuberi look around for a shelter against the cold, dark night that is rapidly drawing near.
The dead trees provide no shelter from the wind and the rocks seem too creepy to sleep near. Zuberi seems to look in a specific direction all the time, but the snow, the fog and the whiteness of the ground make it difficult to distinguish anything. He seems a bit annoyed, stops his horse and starts staring around into the rapidly darkening surroundings.

Kanoa halts as well and looks deep into the grey fog. He notices the lack of any sound other than the wind. A few motionless ravens sit quietly in a dead tree. The snow dampens all noises and the irregular gusts emphasize the eeriness of this desolate place.

Suddenly Kanoa hears a faint crowing sound emerging from somewhere far in front of them. They look at each other.
Zuberi briefly points to the ravens in the tree nearby and continues to glace around. Doubtfully, Kanoa moves his hood aside, holds his head a bit askew and listens carefully.
His effort is not in vain. Once again he hears crowing coming from the grey fog in front of them. This makes the boy immediately yell out the name he's given the young rook. After a few short crowing sounds, the little black rook emerges from the mist and snow. It skims over them, turns and flies back to where it came from.
Kanoa immediately bends down on his horse, briefly hums and has the horse rapidly follow Kra. Zuberi sees Kanoa's hasty departure and he immediately follows the boy.
They cannot yet see that the black rook is flying towards an old ruin on a hillside. It is partly snowed in, but is sufficient as a shelter for the upcoming night.

Meanwhile, the castle has become quiet. Baaqir rests in his wagon-house. Most of the guards, knights and servants have gone to their quarters.
In a fairly large room, a grand fireplace illuminates several chairs and a rectangular, wooden table in the center.
King Eadwin and AnZhiMu sit at opposite ends of the table.
In between them stands a large candle, a plate holding a loaf of bread with a few slices cut off, and two mugs.
A painting hangs on the wall. It depicts a young King Eadwin, wearing a golden crown with a black marble. He stands in front of his impressive castle on the mountain.

King Eadwin sits despondently at his end of the table. His elbows are on the table top and his head rests in his hands while he just stares at the shiny wood in front of him.

Frustrated by the king's weakness, AnZhiMu stands up. The sound of the shuffling chair over the stone floor startles not only the king, who now also rises, but Bo as well, who was sleeping in front of the fireplace. The little black dog barks a few times and stands up.
AnZhiMu looks desperately into the king's eyes while she repeatedly points to the north. King Eadwin now seems to understand that she expects him to rescue Luzette.

The king gently puts a hand on her shoulder and nods. He then walks to the door, opens it and yells a command as he enters the hall. AnZhiMu follows him into the hall, which has been brought back to its original state with the large wooden table in the center.
She holds the door open for a moment, allowing Bo to exit as well, and then gently closes the door behind her. When she turns around to the hall, she sees several knights appear and gather around the table. While King Eadwin stands at the head of the table, he blinks his eyes and quickly nods towards AnZhiMu, who quietly leaves, followed by the little black dog.
She is obviously tired and retires to her room for the night. A female servant opens a door for her and both AnZhiMu and Bo enter the bedroom.

AnZhiMu looks around and takes a few small pillows from the bed. Then she carefully lays them on the floor in the corner of the room.
While she looks at the little black dog, she points at the pillows and softly claps the other hand against her thigh a few times. Bo stops sniffing around, playfully looks up and, after AnZhiMu clearly points at the corner one more time, obediently lies down on the pillows.

AnZhiMu smiles and walks to the bed. Slowly and softly she sweeps her hand over the bedspread and sits down. She takes off her shoes and slowly lies down, flat on her back with her hands over each other at her waist.

Bo sits up and hears the lady sigh. Each breath becomes slower and finally, her steady, slow breathing indicates that AnZhiMu has fallen into a deep sleep. The little dog now silently stands up and wags its tail while it sniffs around the room. Bo notices a window above a chest. Before it jumps onto the chest, Bo anxiously looks at AnZhiMu, who is now sound asleep.

Once on the chest, Bo walks to the windowsill and pushes the window open a little bit further. The little black dog turns around to look at the sleeping lady one more time before it quietly looks at the ground outside, which is partially covered in a thin layer of snow.

Then it jumps out the window. After it lands outside, the dog shakes itself and looks around. It is almost dark and it is still snowing a little bit. The black dog starts sniffing around again and soon approaches the empty courtyard.

While it softly barks and increases its pace, it soon walks in front of the stairs to the enormous wooden entrance doors, which are now closed. Its sniffing leads the little dog off to the north. As it approaches open terrain, Bo starts running into the dark, snowy night, following the path of the evil giants, who took Luzette, as well as the path of Kanoa and Zuberi.

While AnZhiMu sleeps, King Eadwin and his men finish deliberating. When the king stands up, all the other men follow suit.

The king shouts and holds his fist up high towards the north, and his actions are is promptly repeated by the others. It seems they will leave for the north in the morning.

The knights return to their quarters and the king walks towards a doorway behind the throne. But suddenly, he stops, turns around, and then proceeds to AnZhiMu's bedroom. He knocks very softly and listens carefully.

As he hears no response, he slowly opens the door a little bit and peaks through the opening to see AnZhiMu soundly asleep on the bed.

With a gentle smile on his face, he slowly closes the door and walks past the throne. He stops once more, lays a hand on the throne, looks around in the hall, sighs, and proceeds to his quarters.

In the east, the sultan, Keiji and the three guards enter the grounds of the sultan's palace just before the darkness of the evening falls over the land.
As the sultan halts his horse, he is immediately surrounded by guards and servants, who escort him into the palace.
The guards lead their horses to the stables and Keiji quietly follows them.
Most of the guards walk to the palace but one remains. Since all the guards wear cloaks and scarves that obscure their faces, it is difficult to distinguish one from another.

The guard in front of Keiji now removes the uniform's headscarf and Keiji does not seem surprised to see a young female face revealed. He smiles and speaks her name, "Nabhitha". She returns the smile and then turns around. They walk towards the palace alongside each other.
When Nabhitha enters the palace, she is followed by a somewhat cautious Keiji, who tries to hide himself a little behind her as they walk between tall pillars towards an enormous, domed palace hall.

The sultan, surrounded by guards and servants, has already entered the palace and takes his seat at the end of the hall on a platform between two elder advisors and a number of female servants dressed in colorful, shimmering silk and gauzy veils. They are sitting on a raised platform surrounded by little tables with exotic fruits, breads and various bottled beverages.
The big wooden chair the sultan is reclining in is surrounded by red and purple pillows, spread all over the platform.
Obviously glad to be back at home, the sultan rests his bare feet on one of the pillows and sees Nabhitha and Keiji approaching the platform.

He sits back, takes a deep breath, and sighs audibly. He grumbles a bit while both his hands grasp the ends of the chair's armrests.

As Nabhitha walks towards the sultan, Keiji notices that the other guards and servants bow towards her. When she stops in front of the sultan, Nabhitha bows slightly and gently smiles. This seems to soften the sultan's mood and he gestures for her to sit at his side.

Nabhitha reaches out one hand behind her and turns her head towards Keiji. But she is surprised because she does not see Keiji right behind her, as she had apparently expected. He is some distance further back, somewhat hidden behind a pillar.

When Nabhitha smiles and waves for him to come, Keiji slowly approaches the platform and bows before the sultan, who seems fairly relaxed now.

As Keiji sits down near Nabhitha, the sultan claps his hands twice in order to have some servants bring food and drinks.

The sultan takes a silver plate and places several slices of meat and some fruit on it. He then moves his hand towards Nabhitha and Keiji to have the servants offer them food as well. Together, they all start eating their dinner in the palace hall.

After a while, when most of their food has been eaten, Keiji looks at Nabhitha a few times, whispers Luzette's name and nods towards the sultan. The sultan puts the last piece of fruit in his mouth just as Nabhitha moves a bit closer to him. She looks him in the eyes, mentions Luzette's name and subsequently points at Keiji and then at the guards at the other end of the hall, and then looks straight at the sultan again.

Keiji looks up and watches how the sultan briefly moves his hand over Nabhitha's head and sighs. When he looks at Keiji, the young man respectfully looks down.

Awaiting the sultan's decision, Nabhitha notices Keiji's tension and the sultan's daughter touches his hand briefly, yet comfortingly.

Meanwhile, Kra has led Kanoa and Zuberi through the snowy wastelands to an old ruin.
Fragments of an ancient castle stand out in front of a snowy hill. Kra lands on a piece of wall, crows a few times and waits for Zuberi and Kanoa. Although the wind is bitterly cold, both boys seem happy. Kanoa is pleased to see his feathered friend again and Zuberi is relieved they have found the shelter he was searching for.

Kanoa stops his horse and intends to dismount but Zuberi shakes his head and gestures for Kanoa to follow him as he proceeds over some flat, old stairs that are half snowed in. There his horse is situated behind a wall, out of the harsh wind.
Zuberi dismounts his tired horse and immediately starts taking the bags off of the saddle. Kanoa carefully dismounts. As soon as he has both feet on the ground, the rook spreads its wings, floats down and flaps its wings while it lands on Kanoa's outstretched arm. Kanoa smiles and with his other hand he grabs a piece of bread and holds it in front of the rook's beak.
Kra picks at the bread and enthusiastically swallows large pieces at once. While swallowing the rook is wildly moving its head and neck. Kanoa smiles and gently moves his finger through the bird's neck feathers until a short yell of Zuberi disturbs his wandering thoughts.

The boy turns around to Zuberi and is surprised to see his companion rapidly spreading out a large canvas cloth as the bottom part of their shelter for the night.
Zuberi nods towards the sack beside his horse. Kra flies back to sit on the wall and Kanoa opens the sack, takes out a few pieces of rope and starts pulling out a big package.
Zuberi stands up and assists Kanoa. The package is a large piece of canvas cloth which will serve as a tent.

As they unpack and unfold the canvas together, Kanoa notices how fast it is getting dark now. As soon as they finish securing the canvas tent with the ropes, Zuberi picks up the empty sack, briefly looks at Kanoa and disappears into the tent.

Kanoa looks up at Kra and fetches a small piece of dried meat and holds it up. The little rook turns its head and flies to Kanoa's arm. It snatches the piece of meat and wildly shakes it around in its beak a few times before it laboriously swallows the whole piece at once.

It then turns its head to look at Kanoa, who strokes the bird gently. The boy holds up his arm as he sees the bird spreading its wings. The rook crows once and flies into the dark sky. Kanoa's eyes follow the rook until it vanishes into the night. He picks up the remaining bag, bends down and enters the tent.

It is dark in the tent but Zuberi takes out a small decorated metal box they got from Baaqir and opens it. Kanoa watches him carefully remove a small piece of wood fiber from the box and spread it on the open metal cover. Zuberi then takes two pieces of flint out of the box and hits them a few times together until the sparks create a small fire in the fluff on the cover.

He points at a few wooden sticks in the box and looks at Kanoa. While the boy takes a stick and lights it above the small, already dimming flames, Zuberi takes a small lantern out of the bag and opens it. He holds it towards Kanoa, enabling the boy to light it with the flame on the stick.

Zuberi smiles as he places the small burning lantern on the floor. He opens the tent and tosses out the ashes. He then closes the metal box, puts it in the bag and sits back.

Kanoa blows out the stick and takes some food out of the bag, which he gently lays on the canvas floor before he sits down. They briefly look at each other.

Outside the tent, the wind howls around the ruins where they are camping. The lantern's flame flickers inside the tent as they silently eat.

When they have finished, Zuberi takes two big carrots out of the bag and hands one to Kanoa, who looks a bit puzzled.
Then the boy frowns as he sees Zuberi leave the tent. He peeks through the opened tent cloth and sees Zuberi walk to his horse and hold up the carrot for the animal. Kanoa follows him and feeds the carrot to his horse while he gently strokes its mane.
The wind makes Kanoa briefly shiver and Zuberi gestures for him to return to the tent. Kanoa walks back to the tent and stoops down to climb inside. For a moment, he looks up into the dark sky. The clouds are breaking, allowing him to see some parts of the starry sky and the rising moon in the east.

Keiji and Nabhitha are also watching the rising moon as they walk back across the courtyard of the sultan's palace towards the stables. In the stables Keiji sighs as he sweeps his hand over the back of his horse and looks at Nabhitha, who just silently smiles in an attempt to ease her friend's mind.
They embrace each other before Nabhitha returns to the palace and Keiji walks to his quarters for the night. He enters a building attached to the stables and turns around. Before he closes the door, he looks up at the sky towards the north.

As the night grows colder, Bo is still running. The little dog is following the track of Kanoa and Zuberi, heading towards the barren wastelands to the north.
But it seems Bo is not alone. A black and grey wild boar, at least four times bigger than Bo, follows the dog from a distance. The boar's presence goes unnoticed because they are traveling against the wind from the north.
As it has stopped snowing, Bo does not seem to have any trouble picking up the trail and runs at a consistent pace towards Kanoa's shelter amongst the ruins in the distance.

Zuberi dims the lantern and then he and Kanoa lie down in the tent, wrapped in their cloaks and the blankets they got from the king. They are almost asleep when Kanoa suddenly hears something and sits up.

This startles Zuberi, who just lifts up his head. He listens for a while, and then shakes his head and grumbles a little before he lies down again and closes his eyes.

Kanoa slowly lies down too but he keeps his eyes open. Just when his eyes are more closed than open, he hears noises once more and sits up again.

When one of the horses whinnies, Zuberi also sits up. Kanoa seems to recognize the sniffing sound around the tent and says "Bo!"

Immediately he hears a few barks outside the tent. While Zuberi turns up the lantern's flame, Kanoa quickly crawls to the tent opening and slides the canvas aside. Bo jumps towards him and Kanoa embraces the little black dog, which intensely wags its tail and sniffs around the delighted boy.

Zuberi smiles warmly and briefly pets the dog before he lies down again and dims the lantern. Kanoa gives the dog some dried meat and instructs it to lie down. After he strokes the dog's back a few times, he lies down as well and pulls a piece of his blanket over the dog.

11. Next Morning

Just as they are about to fall asleep, Bo suddenly sits up and barks. Zuberi grumbles, rolls over and pulls his cloak tighter. Kanoa opens his eyes and can barely see the restless dog in the moonlight filtering through the canvas tent. As he sits up and looks around somewhat sleepily, the little dog barks and steps toward the tent opening, barks again and then steps back.

They are instantly jolted awake by an abrupt, harsh tearing sound, accompanied by an enormous dent in the canvas tent, which is being violently ruptured by what appear to be large teeth.

Kanoa hears a loud growling sound and the stomping of hoofs outside the tent. He grabs Bo while Zuberi crawls under the canvas at the back of the tent to get out. Kanoa sees Zuberi disappear and then hears him yell loudly.

The stomping stops but the growling increases. Kanoa carefully opens the tent and peeks through the opening. He sees Zuberi standing in front of the tent, trying to make himself appear even larger than he already is, while looking straight at a huge, raging wild boar.

The boar growls, paws at the ground and then charges towards Zuberi.

As the running boar puts its head down, aiming its tusks straight at Zuberi, the boy steps aside and grabs the animal's tusks with his hands and yells loudly.

Turning his whole body, he uses the beast's momentum to swing the heavy, squealing animal through the air and toss it against a stone pillar nearby.

Zuberi growls loudly and walks over to the beast lying on the ground.

When it sees Zuberi, the animal stands up unsteadily.

Zuberi growls at it once more and this makes the animal sprint off into the night, probably fearing for its life.
Zuberi turns around and climbs back into the tent. Kanoa, still catching his breath, holds the tent cloth open for him.
Kanoa smiles with relief and his wide eyes reveal his astonishment and deep respect for the strength and cunning of his companion. Zuberi just briefly smiles back, a little proud, and rearranges some parts of the tent cloth before he lays down again, as do Kanoa and Bo.

Kanoa can just see the silhouette of the sleeping dog against the tent cloth, which is slightly lit by the moonlight and its reflection off the white landscape around them.
Kanoa takes a deep breath and sighs once more before he slowly closes his eyes and gradually falls asleep.
The wind continues to blow around the ruins and the tent they are sleeping in. The clouds are now breaking apart and reveal the stars and rising moon in the east.

The sinister, cloaked man is on his way to the north as well and now travels steadily over the wastelands.
Because of the strong wind on this cold night, he holds his cloak tightly with one hand. Although the wind has driven away most of the fog, it now obscures the man's view by blowing snow over the ground in front of him. Therefore, as the man passes the ruins at some distance, he cannot see the tent hidden behind a piece of the ruin's wall on the hill.

While Zuberi softly snores, the little dog next to him is obviously reliving the day in its dreams. Every now and then it moves slightly and makes some sniffing noises. Similarly, Kanoa's mind slowly swirls into a dreamy state.

Kra flies before him. He follows the rook until it turns around and points its beak upwards while it holds the black marble.
Kanoa reaches out his hand and as soon as he grabs the marble, the rook is gone and he finds himself in the cottage, sitting at the table with Luzette, Keiji and AnZhiMu, into whose reaching hand he drops the marble.

As he looks into the woman's eyes, she holds the marble up high and just stares at it. When Kanoa looks up as well, he sees the shiny black marble in another hand, held up in a dark, dusty room.
Looking down, he sees it is Baaqir holding the marble and he now seems to be in Baaqir's place. Luzette stands in the doorway, reaching out her hand.
While he is staring at the girl's face, Keiji and Zuberi appear behind her, one on each side. King Eadwin stands further away and when Kanoa looks around, they are all in the castle's hall.
Kra comes flying in, straight toward the marble, which now rests on a pillow in the center of the hall.
Luzette runs towards it as well. Just before Kra lands on the pillow and Luzette is about to grab the marble, a giant stone hand slides roughly over the floor at great speed. It crushes the bird and grabs Luzette.

Kanoa turns restlessly in his sleep and Bo wakes up for a moment. The little dog softly howls. Then it yawns, gently sniffs near Kanoa's hair for a moment and closes its eyes.

Kanoa still sees the giant stone hand in his dream. He feels the wind through his hair and when he looks around he finds himself near Zuberi with the rook flying in front of them over bare wastelands, chasing a stone giant.
Then Kra flies to the left and Zuberi goes to the right. Kanoa follows the rocky colossus, who stops after a while and turns around at the edge of a cliff. Luzette stands in front of him and reaches out her hand.
While the rocky giant puts a golden crown, with the black marble in it, on its head with both hands, Kanoa reaches out his hand to Luzette. When he looks up, he sees Kra flying toward the crown.
The rook lands on it, plucks the marble out and flies away towards the cliff. The stone giant tries to grab the rook and turns around.

Then Kanoa hears his name being called, he looks behind
him and feels a rush of air as Kra flies just before him and
presents the marble to him once more.
He reaches out his hand and feels the warmth of the bird.
But when he tries to grab the marble, he feels something wet
on his hand and slowly opens his eyes.

Bo licks Kanoa's reaching hand and then sniffs around his
face. Opening his eyes further, Kanoa pets Bo with his hand,
and sees a big smile on Zuberi's face. His companion sits up.
He is eating some pieces of bread and presents a piece to
Kanoa as well. Kanoa, still a bit confused by his dream, sits
up quite slowly. Zuberi reaches outside the tent with one
hand and retracts it slowly.
When Kanoa stares at Zuberi's closed hand, he suddenly
moves it towards him and throws a small handful of snow
straight into Kanoa's face. Kanoa shouts and grabs his face
with both hands. But then he seems to find it refreshing. He
repeatedly rubs his eyes and face to wake himself up a bit.
Zuberi still smiles, shakes his head a few times and throws a
piece of cloth at Kanoa.

The moon slowly descends in the west and it is almost dawn.
The sky is cloudless and in the east the inevitable sunrise
already lightens the lower part of the eastern sky, turning it a
brilliant light-blue color.

Baaqir slept in his wagon-house on the castle grounds and is
up early. He carefully steps out, closes the top button of his
robe and rubs his hands as he quietly walks towards the
stables. He passes a dormitory for guards and peeks through
a window to see that all is quiet and everyone is still asleep.
He stops at a water pump, bends down, splashes some water
onto his face with his hands and slowly stands upright again.
When he looks around, he sees Zuberi's camel in a stall.
He looks at his wagon-house and subsequently walks to the
camel.

He runs his hand over the camel's neck, mumbles a little and scratches his thin graying beard while he stares for awhile at the animal, which is resting on the straw-covered floor. He then grumbles a bit and walks back to his wagon.
After a while, Baaqir steps out of the wagon-house again with a sack in each hand. He puts down both sacks and closes the door before he walks to the stable where his light-brown horse with a blond mane has spent the night.
Baaqir enters the stable and proceeds to the horse with a smile. He takes a big carrot out of his pocket and mumbles a bit while he presents the treat to the horse and runs his other hand over the neck of the animal for a few moments.

He then returns to the wagon-house, picks up the sacks, walks to Zuberi's camel, and ties both sacks onto the animal.
Baaqir, being somewhat old, and rather frail, cautiously climbs onto the camel's back, sits down and takes the reins.
As he moves the reins, he whispers some things and gently squeezes his knees a few times. The animal stands up, first with its back legs and then with its front legs.
Zuberi's uncle is tipped back and forth a little and has to hold on tight but the camel manages to stand up and Baaqir guides it slowly across the courtyard and to the road that goes down the mountain. Baaqir then brings Zuberi's camel to a smooth gallop and they head off to the south.

Although the courtyard and stables are once again silent, there is some activity in the castle.
The hall is lit by a number of torches. King Eadwin and three knights have just had breakfast and are obviously preparing to leave for the north. They are gathering in the hall and seem packed and ready to go.

When AnZhiMu wakes up, she cannot find Bo anywhere in her bedroom and she goes to the big hall to search for the lost dog. Although it is still very early and there is no sign of any servants, the castle minstrel is walking around and finds AnZhiMu nervously looking around.

He walks up to her and bows a little. He notices her tense smile and her searching eyes. He raises his eyebrows and makes a little bark. The woman now nods and smiles kindly to the minstrel, who instantly starts checking various rooms and places in and around the hall.

While the minstrel searches for Bo as well, AnZhiMu walks to the huge wooden doors in the hall. She anxiously looks around in an effort to find the little black dog.

King Eadwin and three knights now enter the hall. The king looks at his companions, nods and looks outside.

The knights proceed to the stables but the king stops in front of AnZhiMu and looks at her a bit questioningly.

AnZhiMu looks around the hall and bends down a little while she waves her hand a bit above the floor. The king nods, realizing that she is searching for the little dog. He says "Bo" as he puts a hand on her shoulder and looks outside, eastward over the trees towards the cottage.

AnZhiMu smiles for a moment and blinks her eyes before she points her finger north and then looks anxiously at King Eadwin. His subdued smile tries to comfort her, but also reveals he is not without worries himself.

The three knights have already mounted their horses and are now guiding the king's horse to the courtyard. AnZhiMu takes his hand and smiles back at him.

He takes a breath, briefly takes her hand with both of his hands and looks at her. He then turns around and descends the wide staircase towards his horse.

While the stars and the moon are still clearly visible, the bright blue color of the sky in the east announces the approaching dawn. The minstrel looks up and sees AnZhiMu holding up her hand towards the king as he and his knights leave the courtyard for the north to find the evil giants that have absconded with Luzette and the marble.

When the four men ride out of sight, AnZhiMu sighs and returns to the hall.

She hears her name being called by the minstrel, who stands in the doorway of her bedroom, and hastily walks towards him. As she approaches, the minstrel walks inside the room, to the window above the chest.
AnZhiMu watches how he looks outside and points his finger at a few tracks in the snow outside, below the window. Bo clearly went outside through the window during the night.
Because the snow has only covered some corners and parts of the ground, the traces disappear in the courtyard.
The minstrel watches AnZhiMu turn around, walk to a chair, fetch her cape and put it over her arm. He understands that she intends to go home and accompanies her to the hall.

The first servants now appear in the hall. The minstrel walks to one of them and whispers some things. The servant nods and immediately leaves.
The minstrel walks back to AnZhiMu, who stands near the throne and just stares into the big hall. When he sees her staring like that, the minstrel decides not to disturb her. Silently and respectfully, he walks towards the large wooden entrance doors and waits.

Just as the minstrel hears the sound of hoofs, outside in the courtyard, he sees AnZhiMu approaching the entrance and bows a little before her. Then he turns around, moves his arm and opens his hand towards the courtyard. AnZhiMu now smiles and walks through the large wooden doorway.

On the landing outside, the minstrel gently takes the cape from her arm and wraps it over her shoulders.
In the courtyard, a guard holds the reins of a beautiful white and grey horse. When the minstrel looks back into the hall, he sees a female servant approaching with a small bag. She hands it to him while she bows her head a little.
The minstrel smiles, takes the bag and nods his head as well. When he turns around, he sees AnZhiMu is already standing near the horse. He hastily walks to her, puts down the bag, assists her onto the horse, picks up the bag again and hands it to her.

She looks in the bag and takes out a bone for a dog to chew on, wrapped in a cloth. With a smile she looks at the minstrel, who also smiles and blinks his eyes once.
She puts back the bone and sees there is some food in the bag for her as well. She nods thankfully and attaches the bag to the saddle of the horse before she bends down and puts her hand on the shoulder of the friendly minstrel.

While the first rays of the sun hit the eastern side of the forest in the mountains, AnZhiMu sits up and instructs the horse to commence.
The minstrel holds out his hand towards AnZhiMu as she slowly begins her journey down the mountain and through the forest. She heads towards her cottage on the hill, assuming the little black dog has already found its way back there.

Bo, however, is actually leading Kanoa and Zuberi further north. The emerging sun now illuminates the rocky ground they ride over. The small remaining drifts of snow slowly melt and glisten in the early morning sunlight.
Long shadows stretch westward behind each stone and rock formation. Since they have to stay behind the dog, steadily running in front of them, they ride slowly. This gives Kanoa the opportunity to dwell on his thoughts in this surreal scenery, where even the long shadow of the little dog seems monstrous.

The dog gradually slows down as the path on the rocky terrain becomes steeper and narrower and ultimately seems to end. While Bo carefully sniffs around, Zuberi steps off his horse and leads it behind a small rock formation. Kanoa also steps off and accompanies him.
Bo barks in a slightly subdued manner for some time and stands at the end of the path looking down. Zuberi carefully steps towards the dog and crouches down a little. He makes a hushing sound and softly lays his hand on the back of the little dog and looks down.

When Kanoa slowly approaches them and crouches down next to Bo, he sees that the path continues downwards as a rather wide and flat, carved stone stairway alongside the steep cliff they appear to be on.
These stairs end in front of a wooden bridge suspended by many ropes over a deep ravine. The bridge leads to the other side of the ravine, where everything seems to be made entirely of rocks.
On the other side of the bridge, a narrow path continues along the side of another cliff. This path leads to the mouth of a large cave.

"Luzette", Kanoa says as he stands up. Zuberi immediately stretches his arm up and pulls him back down. He hushes Kanoa and points his finger toward the mouth of the cave on the other side of the ravine. There the limping, sinister figure leads his horse on foot over the narrow path along the side of the steep, rocky cliff towards the mouth of the cave.
The younger giant now comes out of the cave's entrance. Zuberi and his young companion see the sinister man leave his horse outside and enter the cave, followed by the somewhat uncertain young giant, who looks at the bridge, the wide stairs and the other side for a moment before he turns around and follows the cloaked man into the dark cave.
Kanoa looks up, a bit shyly, but Zuberi smiles reassuringly for a moment and moves backwards a little. Unsure of what to do, he turns around and looks at the horses near the rocks.
Kanoa looks at Bo and pets the little dog for a few moments before he hears Zuberi sigh. As he moves closer again, frowns and shakes his head. It is clear that they have to go to the cave, but to take a horse over the bridge would attract far too much attention.

Then Zuberi suddenly lies down and peeks over the edge. He sees the older colossus. He is wearing the golden crown and pushing the younger one outside.
He then points to the bridge and seems to be telling him to guard the entrance. The older giant grumbles and goes back inside.

The younger giant now slowly walks to the bridge, stands at
the end of the bridge with both hands on the railing and
looks toward the other side.
Kanoa quietly bends down to observe the younger giant turn
around and sit down on a piece of rock. He obviously intends
to stay there and keeps his eyes on the bridge.

Zuberi and Kanoa look at each other and cautiously crawl
backward. They stand up near the horses, behind the rocks.
Zuberi looks around and stares at another rock formation,
further away from the path. He takes the reins of his horse
and leads it somewhat further away.
Kanoa seems to be deep in his thoughts and remains with Bo
and his horse, close to the flat stone stairs leading to the
bridge. Then the boy feels the outside of the bags tied to the
horse's saddle. He smiles, unties one of the bags and puts it
on the ground. From the bag he fetches a long rope and
starts unwinding one end.

Zuberi comes walking back. He tilts his head a little, looks at
Kanoa and then looks back at the rock formation further
away where he just left his horse.
However, Kanoa proudly shows the rope and the loop he
made. He gestures throwing the rope, pulling it, tying it
around something and, while hanging on the rope, climbing
over the ravine to the other side of the cliff.
Zuberi laughs out loud. This makes Kanoa frown. He drops
the rope and takes Zuberi's arm to lead him back to the end
of the path, where they crouch down together.

Kanoa points at the wooden support beams of the bridge
further down and subsequently points below the bridge on
the other side, where an old, dead tree trunk could serve as a
hook for the rope.
Kanoa looks at Zuberi, who seems to be more serious and
interested now, points at him and subsequently points at a
spot with some rocks a bit higher up.
Then he picks up a stone and pretends to throw it to the
other side, away from the bridge.

He indicates that Zuberi should distract the young giant guarding the bridge and the path to the cave's entrance.

This idea now seems to appeal to Zuberi as he nods his head enthusiastically and looks down the cliff. They slowly retreat to Kanoa's horse and the boy grabs the rope.
Bo has been quite silent since they were watching the giants. Kanoa bends down in front of the black dog and points at Zuberi, who is collecting a few small stones.
The little black dog looks inquisitively at Kanoa, who smiles and gently lays his hand on Bo's head before he stands up and walks to his companion.

Zuberi sees that Kanoa is trying to lead Bo to him. Zuberi fetches a piece of bread out of his pocket and stretches out his hand while he bends down.
Bo's tail, still hanging somewhat low, now wags a bit as the little dog walks to Zuberi. While Bo takes the piece of bread, Kanoa looks at Zuberi and nods while he crouches down and crawls towards the stone stairs leading to the bridge.
Zuberi, staying low above the ground, quietly leads Bo to a higher piece of ground, behind a few boulders. He carefully lays down his collected stones and puts himself in a good throwing position.
Then he cautiously looks over the boulders and sees the colossus, still sitting at the other end of the bridge. He crouches back down and looks at Kanoa, who sits ready with the rope over his shoulder and clearly nods towards Zuberi.
Zuberi sits up, takes a careful look and forcefully throws a little stone over the ravine, far beyond the bridge and the giant. He quickly hides behind the rocks again before the stone even reaches the other side. The stone hits the rocks and skips a few times before it stops.

The giant stands up and curiously walks towards the noises he hears. This immediately triggers Kanoa to silently run down the wide flat stairs.
He hides under the bridge and starts tying one end of the rope to a big wooden beam.

The giant curiously looks over the steep, rocky ground for a while and then turns around again.
Zuberi sees that Kanoa has not yet thrown the rope around the tree trunk on the other side. He cautiously picks up another stone and slowly rises. He waits until the colossus sits down again and then he throws the second stone.

The giant, more alert now, stands up quickly and walks away from the bridge as soon as the stone hits the rocks further away.
Kanoa stands up, swings the rope around a few times and then throws it to the other side. With hardly any sound, the rope hits the rocks just above the tree trunk. Kanoa gently pulls the rope and the loop falls around the trunk.
Kanoa now pulls it until the rope is tight and wraps the remaining part around the wooden beam.
When he looks up at the other side, Kanoa sees that the young giant has once again returned to his spot at the end of the bridge. The bridge blocks the giant's view of the rope underneath.

Kanoa stands up straight and grabs the rope with both hands. He takes a deep breath and wraps his legs and feet over the rope.
Slowly but steadily, he now climbs to the other side, hanging on a rope below the wooden suspension bridge, over the, dark chasm between the two steep cliffs.

As he commences, the rope seems to give a bit more slack every now and then.
The excess rope that Kanoa wrapped around the beam, apparently a little too loosely, is now slowly unwinding.
Zuberi knows that he has to distract the giant again once Kanoa reaches the other side. He sits up a little, stretches out his arm and watches Kanoa nearing the tree trunk on the other side.
But suddenly, the remaining untied rope unwinds and all the extra slack makes the rope slide into a loose curve, abruptly stopping when it catches on the knots.

The rope's movement nearly makes Kanoa fall off. He cries out and, while hanging onto the rope with one hand, his other hand desperately grasps for the tree trunk. Below him, the cliff's wall fades into the seemingly infinite darkness of the ravine.
As Zuberi witnesses this, he retracts his arm and pounds his fist on the rock before him. His reaction makes Bo look up.

12. Caught

Kanoa hangs onto the rope and desperately tries to grab a piece of the trunk. Suddenly, a big, somewhat cold, hand grabs his wrist from above and lifts him up.
The boy lets go of the rope and looks up, into the eyes of the giant, who swings the boy to the path and, fairly gently, releases him.

Zuberi, who struggles to keep the restless little dog quiet, looks over the rocks to the other side and sees Kanoa being guided to the cave's entrance. When Kanoa refuses to walk forward, the colossus pushes him. Kanoa stumbles and falls, somewhat deliberately it seems.
The giant grumbles and reaches out his hand. Kanoa grabs it and stands up. In doing so, he momentarily glimpses the other side of the ravine and is relieved to see Zuberi safely watching from behind the rocks.

As Zuberi's eyes follow Kanoa and the giant disappearing into the cave, he cautiously creeps back and commands Bo to wait with Kanoa's horse. He then swiftly crawls down the stairs and runs across the bridge.
The little dog quietly obeys, keeping its tail down, but it continues sniffing around, behind the boulders and rocks. Bo occasionally peeks at the bridge and the cave's entrance.

Although it is still very early, the wind has blown away most of the fog and clouds, giving the weak sunshine opportunity to gradually illuminate the sky and warm up the morning air.
Kanoa, followed closely by the giant, enters the cave. They walk through a dark tunnel. A few burning torches, mounted along the walls, produce an irregular, orange light.

At the end of the tunnel Kanoa enters a large cavern, with a central fire pit surrounded by some rocks. Next to the fire the larger, more malicious giant stands up and growls. He looks straight at Kanoa and he stomps towards him. Kanoa tries to step back, but a large hand pushing into his back prevents him from doing so. Kanoa's eyes grow large as he sees the marble in the crown on the giant's head.

The angry colossus stumbles over a rock, which rolls against the leg of the dark, sinister figure, who is sitting near the fire. The man grumbles and uses his walking stick to stand up and turn around to see the evil giant ferociously grabbing Kanoa's arm.

When the boy is violently dragged past the sinister, limping man, the man stares into Kanoa's eyes from under his cloak in a very intimidating manner. Then Kanoa hears his name being called out loudly.

It is Luzette's voice. Relieved to know she is still alive, he desperately looks around the cave to see Luzette. She is chained and her head is wounded, but she seems quite excited to see him, as she sits up in a rather dark corner of the cave.

The angry, older colossus flings Kanoa into the same dark corner. Then he turns to his younger brother and grumbles while he points at Kanoa, who is still rolling over the stone floor. The boy only stops when he hits the solid rock wall of the cave. Luzette crawls to him and helps him sit up. Just as Kanoa looks up at Luzette, he is suddenly pulled away by the smaller giant, who winds a chain around his ankle and fastens it to a steel ring that is attached to the floor. For a brief moment, Kanoa and the younger giant look at each other.

The boy then looks around the cave. He sees a pile of firewood and two untidy beds, each in a corner. The beds are not much more than piles of furs and pieces of cloth.

In another corner are a few large jugs, two wagons with large wooden wheels, some barrels and a wooden cage. Various bones are scattered on the floor along all the sides of the messy cave.

The giant mumbles and walks to the central fire pit. His older brother sits down again, picks up a large bone partly covered with meat, and starts gnawing on it greedily, dribbling saliva down his chin.

The golden crown on his massive, balding head almost falls off as he twists his neck to take another bite.

The sinister man, standing near the fire, leaning on his stick, grabs the crown with one hand to prevent it from falling. The eating colossus seems very annoyed when the sinister man touches the crown and growls loudly.

While some pieces of meat fall out of his mouth, he swings the greasy bone around, striking the arm of the cloaked man, who immediately releases the crown and steps back.

Fetching his stick with his other hand, the sinister cloaked man frowns and wipes off his dark, filthy cape before he carefully approaches the giant again.

His eyes restlessly look at the crown as he stops before the older giant, who just wipes his mouth with his arm, tosses aside the bone and stands up. The colossus points to the cave's entrance and yells at his younger brother, who obediently walks outside to guard the bridge again.

While Bo waits on the other side of the ravine, near Kanoa's horse, Zuberi carefully passes the sinister man's horse and very cautiously looks into the cave. As he sees the younger giant rapidly approaching the exit, Zuberi backs away from the cave immediately and rushes back to the bridge.

As he hears the colossus coming out, he jumps under the bridge and hides himself under it. While Zuberi is still catching his breath, the giant passes the dark horse near the cave exit. He walks towards the bridge and stops at the tree trunk, where he pulled Kanoa up, and looks down.

He sees the rope, which is now hanging in a low, loose curve between the trunk and the other side. Zuberi holds his breath and pushes himself against the side of the stone cliff under the bridge.

Finally, he hears the giant walk a few steps back and sit down on a rock, making it impossible for Zuberi to go anywhere without being noticed.

Inside the cave, the sinister man seems to have great interest in the marble as he holds out his hand towards the colossus. But this annoys the giant and he pushes the old, limping man's hand away, almost making him fall.
The angry giant fetches the crown from his balding head and strikes it possessively against his chest a few times. In doing so, the marble is jostled loose and falls on the ground. It bounces a few times and rolls towards the fire pit. It comes to a stop against one of the stones around the fire, just at the foot of the sinister man. His eyes widen and focus on the little black orb as he bends down and picks it up off the floor.
Before the man can even stand up again, the colossus grabs his arm and stares at him, hardly able to suppress his fury. Then he bends down, holds the crown before him and points at the hole where the marble should be.
The sinister cloaked figure looks back at him venomously for a moment before he slowly returns the marble to its place in the crown. The giant immediately pulls the crown away, pushes the marble in place once more, and puts the crown back on his head again.

Kanoa and Luzette watch all of this and see how the angry colossus grumbles and waves his arms. Then he forces the limping, sinister figure to leave.

Outside, the cloaked man emerges from the cave obviously very dissatisfied. He takes the reins of his horse and slowly leads it towards the bridge.
The younger giant near the bridge stands up somewhat startled. He watches the sinister man stoically limp down the path and then over the bridge to the other side.
Still hiding under the bridge, Zuberi sees the shoes of the man and the hoofs of the horse through the ropes and wooden planks.

As they creakingly pass over him, he anxiously keeps himself pressed against the rocks.

When the sinister cloaked man reaches the top of the wide carved staircase and stands on the other side of the ravine, he looks around and then slowly mounts his dark horse.

He slowly rides past the large rocks where Kanoa's horse is tied. Bo has obviously seen the man coming and silently keeps out of sight behind the rocks.

The sinister man adjusts his cape, looks back toward the mouth of the cave and heads southeast.

Zuberi is still hiding underneath the bridge when he hears the older colossus inside the cave yelling for his younger brother, who then walks towards the cave's entrance.

As Zuberi hears the giant finally leaving the bridge, he carefully climbs up, peeks over the rocks and sees him enter the cave. As soon as the coast is clear, he climbs up to the path and rushes over to the entrance. He cautiously enters the cave and crouches down against the wall.

Through the tunnel he sees the two giants standing next to a dying fire in the center of the cavern and he notices the crown with the marble, resting askew on the head of the older giant. Zuberi carefully crawls a bit further into the tunnel and sees Luzette and Kanoa chained in the corner.

Kanoa has his hands on the chain around his ankle, and Luzette seems to be keeping watch. Zuberi slowly crawls closer. He desperately stares at Luzette until she finally sees him, crouched against the cave wall. She opens her mouth but Zuberi immediately puts his index finger to his lips.

Luzette now presses her hand over her mouth trying hard to remain silent.

Her other hand taps against Kanoa's side. He looks at her and follows her glance toward the cave's exit until he sees his companion as well.

Zuberi indicates that he will leave and come back for them later. He briefly smiles at Luzette before he cautiously crawls back out.

Kanoa and Luzette look at each other. Kanoa notices how exited and happy Luzette now seems. This makes Kanoa smile for a moment as well.

Carefully, Zuberi leaves the cave and silently runs over the bridge to the other side. He runs up the wide, stone stairs and stops when he arrives at Kanoa's horse behind the rocks, where he is welcomed by a joyful Bo.
He clearly intends to go for help and tries to explain to the little dog that it has to remain there, hidden behind the rocks with the horse.

Zuberi then walks to the rock formation further away, where he brought his horse earlier. As if the little dog understands what to do, it remains near Kanoa's horse, still standing behind some rocks, close to the wide, flat stone stairs. It barks quietly once as it sees Zuberi turn his horse and ride rapidly off to the south.

The sinister man, who is riding back towards the southeast, suddenly hides behind some rocks. He watches the king and three knights heading north at some distance.
He thoughtfully rubs his hand over his chin and mumbles something before he slowly continues his journey back.

In the cave, the bigger colossus is obviously preparing to leave. He puts a foot on a barrel and tightens the straps of the leather armor on his leg. He then shouts at his younger brother, points at Luzette and Kanoa, and subsequently points at a wagon and the cage, standing nearby. The older, evil giant then grumbles loudly and finally points at the exit.
The young giant moves one wagon aside and then grabs the thick wooden bars of the cage.
He lifts it up and places it on the other wagon, making both its large wooden wheels groan. He then grabs both handles and pulls the cage-wagon closer to Luzette and Kanoa while his brother checks the weapons on his belt.
It holds a knife, a large sword and an enormous whip.

Bo stands on the other side of the bridge and watches the older giant come out of the cave. He impatiently waits for his younger brother, who slowly emerges pulling the cage-wagon, in which Luzette and Kanoa are now imprisoned.

The little dog suppresses an urge to bark and restlessly walks down the stone stairs to the bridge. The wagon slowly proceeds toward the bridge over the narrow path. All of a sudden, Kra comes floating through the air from behind the vehicle. Without a sound, the rook lands on the back of the wagon behind the cage. "Kra", Luzette whispers happily.
The younger giant obviously hears something and turns around. Kanoa immediately starts coughing and moves in front of the little black rook. Kra starts picking and pulling at a metal pin, which serves as a lock for the cage doors.
As the younger giant steers the wagon onto the bridge at a snail's pace, the little rook manages to remove the pin and flies ahead towards the larger and older giant, already halfway across the bridge.

Kanoa immediately opens the doors of the sturdy wooden cage and carefully jumps out of the wagon. While the boy turns around to help Luzette climb out, Kra flies toward the golden crown on the head of the larger giant.
Bo begins barking and running faster, now over the bridge, towards the annoyed colossus, who turns around to look at his brother. The older giant roars immediately as he sees the two prisoners trying to escape. Shouting angrily at his younger brother, he points at the open cage behind him.
Then, seeing the rook flying towards his head, the older giant begins flailing his arms in the air. Despite the wild movements of the colossus, Kra is able to land on the crown.

The rook's wings flap irregularly. It is focused on the marble and picks and pulls at it. The colossus violently waves his hand above his head and eventually hits Kra.
The blow also hits the crown, which falls off his head, bounces on the bridge and starts rolling toward the edge.

The little rook crows loudly, weakly flaps its wings, and then falls into the deep, dark ravine below the bridge.

Bo is trying to run to Kanoa and Luzette as fast as possible, but the crown now rolls a few steps in front of the young dog. Just as Bo tries to run around the obstacle, an enormous foot slams against the dog's side and knocks the little dog backward. Still howling, Bo rolls towards the edge of the bridge and then rolls off. The angry colossus snatches the crown, just before it falls over the edge, and emphatically puts it on his head again as he turns around toward the wagon.

Kanoa, holding Luzette's hand as she steps out of the cage, sees Bo rolling off the edge of the bridge and screams the dog's name. The younger giant suddenly shakes the wagon, making Luzette fall off. Kanoa's firm grip on her hand prevents her from falling too hard onto the stone path.
Suddenly, Bo's snout appears above the edge of the bridge. Hanging precariously by its front paws over the dark abyss, the little dog is desperately trying to climb up with its back legs.
When Kanoa releases Luzette's hand and anxiously looks down at her, he sees the girl suddenly being pulled back. She screams as she slides over the path and is lifted into the air by the larger, evil colossus. He angrily holds her legs with one hand, swings her above the deep ravine and holds her there.

Luzette screams at first, but then just trembles in fear as she sees the big colossus point at the cage and stare wildly at Kanoa. Obediently, Kanoa climbs back into the cage. The angry colossus swings Luzette back into the cage and slowly drops her.
Kanoa tries to smile somewhat reassuring as he looks at her and reaches out his hand. The younger giant ties Kanoa's wrists to one of the bars and does the same with Luzette before he closes the cage's doors.

He binds the doors together with another piece of rope and then continues to pull the wagon.

The young giant follows his older brother, who is already on the bridge again. They ignore the terrified little dog still hanging above the dark depths. Before the wagon passes the little dog, Kanoa, who has been frantically twisting, turning and bending his wrists, manages to free his hands.

Just before they reach the little dog, Kanoa softly yells Bo's name once more and grabs for his belt, which he rapidly unties and pulls off.

He takes the belt in his hand and stretches out his arm between the bars of the cage. When they pass the desperate little dog, Kanoa gently throws the end of his belt just in front of Bo while he holds the other end in his hand.

Bo lunges for the belt a few times and finally succeeds in biting firmly into the leather. As the wagon moves forward slowly, Kanoa carefully pulls the belt, making it possible for the dog, constantly clawing with its hind legs, to ultimately climb over the edge, back onto the bridge. The little dog releases the belt and shakes itself.

The bigger giant waits at the end of the bridge and helps push the wagon up the wide stone stairs. Kanoa pretends he is still tied to the bar. He looks back and sees that the dog is still following them, limping and out of breath.

He grabs some pieces of bread from his pocket and secretly drops them behind the wagon, near a small pool of freshly melted snow. While both giants stop to look around, Kanoa watches Bo recuperate near the pool.

The younger giant looks over the wastelands and notices a dusty trail of some approaching horses, still very far away. He point at it and taps his brother's arm. The elder giant now sees that others are approaching and reflexively adjusts the crown on his head.

He then angrily turns his head and looks at the sloped plateau to the north. His younger brother shakes his head a few times. The elder giant, however, stubbornly grumbles and starts walking up the plateau.

The younger giant shakes his head again, grabs the handles of the wagon and briefly looks at the prisoners before he starts following his brother.
Luzette repeatedly points at her neck with her chin and Kanoa questioningly pulls her necklace once. The young woman nods explicitly while she turns her back to him, enabling the boy to untie her necklace. Luzette sighs impatiently as it takes Kanoa quite a while to untie the necklace and carefully remove it.
He raises his eyebrows as he holds it outside the wagon. Luzette nods again and Kanoa looks around first and then gently throws it right in the center of a small, flat stone along their path. As they now travel further up the sloped plateau, they hope this necklace will be found and let others know where they were taken.

Meanwhile, in the eastern palace, Keiji has woken up early and is already preparing his horse. Nabhitha, disguised in her guard uniform, joins him and takes Keiji back inside the palace to the sultan, who is just eating breakfast at the back of the hall.
Nabhitha walks in rather quickly and stops before her father, who looks up and raises one eyebrow. She points at a few guards, mentions Keiji's and Luzette's name, and tightens her belt, holding a sword on her right side and a knife on the other side.

After some silence, the sultan shakes his head and mumbles something. Then, rather upset, Nabhitha walks off to her personal residence, further down the hall. Keiji modestly looks down as he hears the sultan grumbling a bit.
Nabhitha leads the two guards who were standing in front of her residence back to the sultan. The sultan stands up and sighs, understanding that he cannot prevent Nabhitha from leaving with her own guards.
Nabhitha seems content now and smiles at her father before she turns around. She looks at the guards and into Keiji's restless eyes, and then starts running to the exit, promptly followed by the two guards.

Keiji turns to leave, but suddenly turns back, bows slightly towards the sultan, and then follows the others.
This kind of amuses the sultan and he smiles, gently shaking his head a few times.
The sultan then slowly walks to the courtyard and from there he watches Keiji, Nabhitha and the two guards leave the palace grounds and ride rapidly off to the north.

As they slowly travel up the sloped plateau looming to the north, Kanoa notices that the warm, yellow sunlight and increasingly lush vegetation make the area very different from the wastelands he saw very early this morning. The bumps, rocks and grassy areas, are also making it much harder for the younger giant to pull the cage-wagon uphill. He stops and sighs.
The larger giant turns around to see why his brother has stopped, and then, looking far back in the distance, he sees the king and the knights heading for the bridge.
He grumbles and sighs loudly while he looks at his younger brother, who then looks down the hill as well and sees Luzette and Kanoa also watching the four men on horses nearing the bridge. The giant looks at his older brother, who, though clearly aggravated, just turns around, looks up the sloped plateau and proceeds.

Kanoa tries to untie the rope around Luzette's wrists but the knot seems very tight. While Luzette tries to bend and twist her wrists, Kanoa decides to leave another article behind, since the terrain now contains more trees and bushes.
He fetches a small piece of cloth, a handkerchief, out of his pants pocket and drops it outside the wagon. But not much further away, the giants move the cage-wagon to a grassy area near the steep side of a big rock formation.
Kanoa quickly pretends to be tied as the giants look at them before they leave Luzette and Kanoa behind to walk back downhill a little. The giants hide themselves behind some large rocks and are obviously eager to find out whether they are being followed by the king and his companions, who they just saw close to the bridge further down the slope.

As soon as the giants have left, Kanoa tries to untie the rope securing the cage doors. Finally, he succeeds. He opens the doors and sneaks over to some rocks nearby, where he starts smashing a small rock against a big rock until it breaks into a few pieces. He picks up a sharp piece, rushes back to Luzette and starts cutting the thick rope from the outside of the cage with the sharp-edged piece of the stone.

Meanwhile, Zuberi is still galloping to the south on his horse and has almost reached the settlement where his younger brother lives with his uncle. As he slows down and begins to follow the path leading to the open area in front of the large, round tent, people curiously look up. Some warriors stop their exercises and a few of the children yell.
The children's noises and the barking of a dog seem to have announced his arrival. The guards stand ready as the main tent is already being opened. Zuberi is pleased to see his kind uncle, Baaqir, peeking out through long strands of beads in the tent's entrance.
While Baaqir slowly comes outside, followed by Zuberi's younger brother, Zuberi smoothly dismounts the royal horse, leads it to a trough and walks towards them.

Baaqir looks at him questioningly and asks about Luzette and Kanoa, pronouncing their names with his low voice.
Zuberi looks at his uncle and lays a hand on his shoulder. He then turns to his younger brother, who keeps staring at him enquiringly, lays his other hand on his brother's shoulder and guides them both towards the tent, where Baaqir's brother, Zuberi's other uncle, stands waiting. They proceed into the tent and sit down on the many colorful carpets and pillows spread over floor.
Baaqir walks to the side of the tent, fetches some mugs from a decorated wooden table, places them on a metal tray and prepares some drinks.
It is obvious Zuberi wants to return to the cave to rescue Luzette and Kanoa as soon as possible. Baaqir nods as he brings the tray to them and his young nephew almost looks excited to participate in this mission.

When Zuberi points at the warriors practicing with spears outside the tent, his other uncle, the current chief of the tribe, shakes his head, refusing to send warriors with them to the north. Silently, they drink and look at each other.
Then Baaqir grumbles softly, stands up and walks out of the tent, followed by the others. In front of the tent, Baaqir turns to Zuberi and points behind a few tents further away. They both look in the direction of the camels and cattle near the lake. Zuberi looks at him, slowly starts smiling and nods.
Baaqir then whispers something to his younger nephew, who seems to be very pleased and runs to another, fairly large, round tent with a shelter above the entrance.
Baaqir now steps towards his stern brother and mumbles a few things. His brother frowns and rubs his chin before he slowly walks to another group of tents, followed by Baaqir, who seems to be happy that his brother will finally cooperate in some way.

After some time, Baaqir returns, leading two horses. His brother comes back, followed by two tribal warriors on horses. Zuberi's brother comes out of his tent. He has exchanged his slippers for leather boots and is now wearing a cape. He walks, somewhat proudly, over to Baaqir, who hands him the reins of one of the horses. They mount the horses and turn around to see Zuberi, approaching. He is leading not only his horse but also two rhinoceroses, each wearing a decorated leather collar with rings on the sides.

This draws the attention of all the surrounding attendees, who start shouting enthusiastically.
To see his large and intimidating brother leading such a fine horse and these grand rhinoceroses impresses Zuberi's younger brother, who also shouts loudly a few times.
This initiates many others to gather joyfully around the open central area.
Amid this cheerful scene, Zuberi mounts his horse and leads both rhinoceroses out of the settlement, followed by two guards, his younger brother and his old, loyal uncle Baaqir.

The other uncle remains very stoic, but he does lift his arm towards the caravan as it leaves the settlement for the north. Although the massive rhinoceroses slow the pace a little, Zuberi leads them fairly rapidly over the dry, southern landscape.
They then travel near the forested hills and mountains, on their way to the northern wastelands.

While the sinister, cloaked man is traveling back to the eastern village, he sees AnZhiMu, still far away, slowly riding the white and grey horse down the path in the mountains, on her way home.
As the evil man crosses the path that leads to the cottage, he stops his horse and turns onto the path. He grumbles and bends down a little as the he slowly approaches the cottage.
The dog guarding the cottage starts barking at the open window when the man stops and slowly dismounts. His black horse restlessly stamps its hoofs on the ground.

The man fetches something out of his saddle bag and then limps fearlessly towards the open window, straight to the barking dog and suddenly clamps his hand around the dog's mouth and forces it to swallow something.
The dog howls softly, licks its mouth a few times, retreats and walks, somewhat unsteadily, back to its basket, where it practically collapses against its offspring and closes its eyes.

The evil man pushes the door open and enters the cottage. He looks around and sweeps his hand over the cape on the wall, over the table and the chest, and finally stops before the fireplace, where he fetches the kettle and removes the cover. He turns his head to the door once, before he takes a small flask from his pocket and releases a few drops into the kettle.

He then turns around, limps back outside and closes the door. He mounts his horse and then heads back down the path.

When he is again at the crossing with the road to the east, he stops, turns around and looks at the mountain path. He watches AnZhiMu now approaching the cottage.
He grumbles somewhat self-righteously before he turns his horse to the east and leaves. He rides fast past the village and on towards the eastern palace.
After a while, AnZhiMu arrives home and stops the horse in front of the high barn behind the cottage. She dismounts carefully, gently leads the white and gray horse to the trough and removes the little bag that she got from the minstrel at the castle before she left early this morning.
When she walks to the door, she curiously looks at the window and bends her head a little, as she obviously expected the mother dog or Bo to welcome her.
After she opens the door, she notices the dog, sleeping between its two young dogs in the basket. She silently removes her cape, puts down the little bag, walks towards the fireplace and lights the fire under the kettle.

After she picks up the mugs from the table and takes them away, she crouches down by the dogs and sighs with a little smile as she sees the little puppies looking up and the mother dog fast asleep. Although it seems strange that the dog is so sound asleep, she lets it rest and briefly pets all the dogs in the basket.
Then she stands up, walks to the door, goes outside and returns with some wood. She lays a few pieces in the stove, and puts some on the side. The little water in the kettle soon makes a bubbling sound and she gets her mug, fetches the kettle and prepares some tea.

The troubled AnZhiMu slowly sits down at the table and notices the bag and cape Kanoa left yesterday a bit hidden in a corner.
She picks up her hot mug of tea with both hands. She drinks and sighs. As she takes another sip, she suddenly feels unwell. She drops the mug, which falls on its side on the table, pushes back the chair and tries to walk to her bedroom. Unable to walk, she falls to her knees.

As the poor woman crawls desperately over the floor past the dogs, the mother dog remains still while the younger dogs, Bo's siblings, stand up and howl softly.

13. To the Top

The king and the three knights, all armed with swords and wearing heavy, decorated leather armor around their chests, approach the bridge. They notice Kanoa's horse which is still standing behind the small rock formation.
One of the knights dismounts, takes his sword and walks down to the bridge. He sees the rope hanging under the bridge and looks up at the king, who nods and gestures for another knight to accompany the first one down to the bridge, before the king also dismounts.

The two knights carefully walk over the bridge and cautiously proceed over the path to the cave entrance. They disappear into the cave, out of the king's sight. While the third knight keeps guard, the king walks to the spirited horse that Kanoa chose yesterday, and guides it over to his own horse.
King Eadwin walks a bit uphill, anxiously looking at the cave every now and then. He notices that these northern lands seem to end here alongside this dark ravine under the bridge.
The king turns around and sees that the only path further is uphill alongside the ravine. Looking up at the wide plateau in front of him, the king notices that, as far as he can see, it looks as if a massive piece of the flat, rocky ground before him has been torn loose and lifted up askew.
Looking back at the bridge and the ravine on his left, the king realizes that he is now standing on a wide, rocky plateau, going slightly, yet steadily, uphill. It seems to fade into the far, hazy northern horizon.

The two knights finally emerge from the cave and clearly shake their heads.

Somewhat disappointed, King Eadwin wanders a bit further up the hill. Suddenly, he stops and yells. He bends down and picks up the necklace Luzette and Kanoa left there as a marker. When the other knight comes over, the king holds it up and repeatedly says "Luzette" and they look up the slope to the north.

The king returns to the horses and shows the necklace to the other two knights, who are returning from the bridge, and he points up the plateau. They all mount their horses and continue further uphill. One knight leads Kanoa's horse with them.

King Eadwin looks up when he suddenly hears a familiar crowing sound. Kra has obviously managed to fly out of the ravine and, up in the sky in front of them, the rook descends in circles and finally lands, out of their sight, on top of the cage wagon. Kanoa, still scraping at the rope holding Luzette in the cage, looks up at the blue-eyed rook happily surprised.

The king and the knights quickly ride towards the distant area where they saw the rook descend.

Further up on the sloped plateau, Bo is still following the wagon's trail. The little dog creeps between the bushes and behind various boulders, scattered along the sides of the terrain, as he carefully passes the two hiding giants.

They are unhappily watching the king and his knights, who are rapidly approaching from further downhill.

The little dog, still limping, manages to get to the wagon. Luzette and Kanoa are glad to see the dog and Kanoa smilingly pets it a little, but quickly continues to scratch the sharp stone over the rope, trying to free Luzette from the cage.

Luzette gasps when she hears the giants growling and sees them down the hill collecting many stones, as they hide behind rock formations and bushes.

Kanoa looks up and sees two knights riding uphill at great speed ahead of the king and the third knight.

As soon as they are close enough, both giants appear and start throwing large stones at them, roaring ferociously.

Both knights are hit hard by the stones and fall off their horses. The king stops his horse, which tramples its front feet in the air and whinnies.

The bigger colossus takes out his whip. He swings it back and then towards King Eadwin. The king is struck hard in the face and falls off his horse. The remaining knight tries to turn around but the whip wraps around his leg and he is violently pulled off his saddle onto the ground.

The king looks up confused. He feels his face and discovers a deep gash running from his cheek to his jaw.

The older giant smiles maliciously and gestures for his younger brother to stay with the king and knights to watch them. With a rather satisfied grumble, he then turns around towards the wagon.

Kra crows and flies off, circles a few times higher up in the sky and finally leaves towards the southeast.

Luzette desperately bends and twists her wrists, while Kanoa stands behind the cage, still anxiously working on the fraying rope. As the last piece of rope finally breaks, Luzette sighs nervously and unwraps the thick rope.

Bo, feeling a bit better now, suddenly stands up on its hind legs and starts barking loudly. When Kanoa looks up, he sees the older colossus angrily pounding towards them. He looks back and sees Luzette has finally loosened the rope and is now stepping through the doors of the cage.

The ferocious colossus raises his fist, and charges straight at the doors of the cage. Kanoa steps back and screams wildly. He shakes his head, and waves his arms for Luzette to move away from the doors. Startled, Luzette steps back just before the giant's fist slams against the cage doors.

As the cage rolls off the trembling wagon onto the ground, the wooden bars screech and creak.

Luzette screams and holds on tightly to a few of the bars. Kanoa sees Bo disappear into the foliage and instinctively follows the dog, diving into the bushes as well.

After adjusting the golden crown with the marble on his head, the giant lifts up the cage with both hands, frowns and glares at Luzette while he takes a deep breath.
Luzette presses herself against the other side of the cage and curls herself up tightly when the colossus utters a terrifying roar, right in front of the cage. She closes her eyes as his foul breath blows through her hair.

The colossus puts down the cage and moves his hand wildly through the bushes, crushing a few of them. Bo has already led Kanoa to a safer spot, behind a few large boulders. From there they can see the king and the knights lying injured on the ground. They try to sneak behind the younger giant through the bushes, in order to help King Eadwin and the knights.

Unable to find Kanoa in the bushes, the furious giant drops the cage holding a terrified Luzette back on the wagon and yells at his younger brother to have him return to the wagon as well.
Kanoa ducks down as the younger giant turns around and obediently walks towards his angry brother. The boy now sees the injured king and knights trying to stand up and he cautiously crawls towards them.
After the older giant finishes retying the rope around the cage doors, he grumbles angrily at his brother, who just looks down a little.
The bigger giant adjusts the crown on his head, looks up at what seems to be the highest part of the plateau they are on, and stubbornly starts walking uphill again.
When he turns around after some time and sees his brother still standing there with the wagon and Luzette, he screams angrily at his younger brother once more and pounds his foot before he continues.

Luzette watches how the younger brother sighs, picks up both handles of the wagon and slowly follows his colossal brother from a distance.

When Kanoa approaches King Eadwin and helps him stand up, the king tries to smile and asks about Luzette.
Kanoa points at the wagon, commencing further uphill, and indicates that the girl is still held prisoner by the giants.
"Zuberi?", the king asks subsequently.
Kanoa shrugs his shoulders, moves his lower lip up for a moment and looks down the hill at the widening terrain behind them to the south.

The three knights slowly stand up, and brush the dirt off their clothes. Limping somewhat, they gather around the king and Kanoa. They briefly deliberate and then walk back to their horses.
When Kanoa sees that they have brought his horse, he walks towards it with a smile. Suddenly, he stops halfway and walks a bit to the side.
He bends down and picks up the handkerchief that he had dropped earlier. He returns to King Eadwin and hands him the piece of cloth. King Eadwin looks up and nods gratefully as he accepts it. He briefly looks at it, frowns for a moment, and then presses it against the wound on his face.

Kanoa proceeds to his horse. Before he mounts the noble steed, however, he crouches down next to Bo, who is still following him. He runs his hand gently over the little dog's head a few times.
The boy starts humming softly as he stands up and grabs the reins of the horse. He lays his hand on its neck, and then, carefully, mounts the graceful animal.
Bo decides to take a different path through the bushes as Kanoa approaches the others. They look up the narrowing plateau but seem unsure how to proceed.

Kanoa suddenly hears Kra crowing from behind him. He immediately turns around and yells the rook's name.

As he looks further down the plateau behind them, he now sees four people on horseback approaching rapidly. The riders have been lead by the rook, which flies high in front of them. Kanoa squints for a moment and then is sure he recognizes Keiji on his horse. He immediately turns to the king and pronounces Keiji's name hopefully.

As Kra flies over them and Keiji, Nabhitha and the guards come closer, the king and his companions turn their horses towards the arriving reinforcements.
Kanoa carefully dismounts, walks a few steps, stretches out his arm and waves it back and forth. When they arrive, Keiji and Nabhitha stop their horses in front of King Eadwin and bow their heads briefly while the guards remain behind them. The king and the knights respond with a gentle bow as well. Then Keiji swings off his horse, walks to Kanoa and asks about Luzette. Kanoa points behind the king and the knights, further up the plateau, where they can just see the giants disappearing behind trees and large boulders, in some kind of bend in the path higher up.
Keiji sighs and asks about Zuberi. Once again, Kanoa shows that he does not know where his companion currently is. He turns around and points down at the bridge near the cave and subsequently looks further south.

They decide to rest and recuperate before they all continue further up the hill to follow the giants and Luzette. One of the knights unties a bag from his horse's saddle, opens it and holds it before King Eadwin, who grabs a piece of bread out of the bag. He then walks over to a big stone and sits down. The knight offers some bread to everyone and as Kanoa takes his first bite, he sees Kra returning from higher up the plateau.
The rook approaches them crowing. Kanoa raises his arm and smiles. All the others look up and see the young, black rook land on the boy's arm and begin pecking at a piece of bread Kanoa holds in front of it. Kra eats some bread, crows once and then quickly flies off again. The rook gradually fades into the bright sky below the sun.

Meanwhile, a watchman in a tower near the eastern palace sees the cloaked, sinister man riding toward the palace and alarms the other guards. The cloaked man slows down as he continues through the large gate because several guards block his way and soon practically surround him, holding up their swords and spears.

The sinister man growls and slowly dismounts his black horse. He leans on his walking stick and watches the sultan, followed by some other guards, approaching.

The guards open the circle around the unexpected visitor to let the sultan through. The sultan resolutely walks straight to the cloaked man, who bends down, in an exaggerated manner, still leaning on his cane.

As the intimidating cloaked man rises very slowly, the sultan questionably frowns and then severely stares at the man before him.

The sinister man raises his walking stick and points it at the palace, indicating that he wants to accompany the sultan inside. The sultan looks doubtful, but turns around, nods at his guards and walks back into the palace. The cloaked, sinister man follows, surrounded by guards, cautiously keeping their eyes on him.

Although the sultan does not seem to appreciate the visit, he still gestures for a servant to prepare refreshments for the cloaked guest.

As they proceed into the palace, everyone suddenly looks up and a certain silence falls over the big hall. The silence is only disturbed by the irregular footsteps of the men on the marble stone floor and an irregular ticking of the walking stick.

Inside the palace, the sultan proceeds to a table in a corner and sits down. A servant places a plate with a few small pieces of bread and meat on the table and another servant puts a filled jug and an empty cup on the table.

The sultan pours some water in the cup and places it in front of the sinister man, who is just sitting down slowly.

The sultan looks rather expectantly at the man, who looks at the guards around them and shakes his head. The sultan sighs audibly and instructs his guards to take some distance. The cloaked and sinister figure now starts mumbling and obviously explains about the crown and the marble. He then gestures putting an imaginary crown on the sultan's head.
The alert guards promptly step closer but the sultan hushes them and motions for them to step back. When the sultan mentions AnZhiMu's name questioningly, the cloaked figure laughs villainously and waves his scarred hand away above the table a few times.
With a skeptical look on his face, the sultan takes a deep breath and scratches his beard. He stands up and turns to his guards. But he remains silent as he once more looks back at the man, who is eating voraciously and spilling water as he guzzles it out of the cup. The sultan sighs indecisively and looks at his guards again.

All the snow has vanished in the morning sun. As the terrain gets higher, more foliage and trees seem to wrap around the light-colored boulders scattered between grassy areas.
The larger colossus, who has constantly been wearing the gold crown with the black marble, leads his brother uphill.
The oblique plateau gradually narrows as they get higher.
Further up the plateau, there is a wide path with flat rocks and grassy areas in the middle.
There are numerous trees next to the wide path and various jagged rocks jut out of the ground randomly along the sides.

Luzette, who is still in the cage on the wagon, keeps looking back, hoping to see her rescuers.
As she looks towards where the giants are taking her, Luzette can see beyond the edge of the plateau and she silently stares at the snowy mountains, far away in the north.

While two of the knights stand up after the short break, Kanoa watches how King Eadwin carefully dabs his drying wound with the handkerchief.

He curiously stares at the piece of cloth for some time and then carefully puts it away. King Eadwin looks at Kanoa, who smiles briefly and starts walking towards his horse, followed by Bo. The king stands up and looks at the others, who are now all preparing for the ride further up the plateau.

Kanoa, now sitting on his horse, looks at the young, limping dog. Then he bends down as far as he can and calls its name. The little dog jumps up and carefully holds onto Kanoa's sleeve with its teeth and scratches his boots with its hind legs. With a smile, Kanoa pulls Bo onto the saddle in front of him and holds the little dog steady with one hand.
As the king mounts his horse, two knights slowly start riding further up the plateau. The other knight escorts the king and Kanoa, who are followed by Keiji, Nabhitha and the eastern guards.

After a while, before they reach the bend in the path, Keiji briefly shouts, stops his horse and clearly indicates that everyone should halt. The knights, riding in front of them, turn around and see Keiji dismount. Nabhitha and the eastern guards also step off their horses and look at Keiji.
He gestures that it is not wise to travel on horseback any further in the middle, open parts of the narrowing plateau. He points to the sides, where trees, bushes and large boulders allow sufficient opportunities to hide their presence and fend off any attack.

King Eadwin nods approvingly and gestures for the three knights to go to the left side of the plateau, where trees, rocks and foliage provide more cover. The knights dismount and lead their horses to some grassy areas on the left side.
Keiji, Nabhitha and the guards guide their horses away from the large pieces of bald rock and grass in the middle to the right side of the plateau, where they cautiously disappear between the boulders and bushes.

Kanoa sighs, somewhat relieved, as he guides Bo back to the ground and dismounts.

The black dog starts sniffing around immediately and obviously smells the giants' trace, since it barks softly and looks at the ground in front of them. Keiji immediately hushes it from behind some bushes.
This makes the little dog playfully run to him. Keiji frowns and bends down to calm Bo down. He grumbles when he sees how this amuses Nabhitha, and her brief laughter further interrupts the silence.

Kanoa is not sure whether to follow the black dog and Keiji, the king or to continue ahead on his own.
For now, he decides to remain somewhat behind the king and the knights, as he leads his horse near their horses and walks to the left side of the plateau, where he hides himself in the bushes near them.
They all now watchfully continue their chase, spread out and hidden, on both sides of the plateau, close to a bend in the path further uphill. Beyond this bend, further up the slope the larger colossus now stops. He sees that he has chosen a path, that seems to stop abruptly further up this cliff.
This last piece of the narrowing plateau is surrounded by bushes, various rock formations and a few trees on both sides. He grumbles, extremely displeased, and turns around. He sees the younger giant exhaustedly parking the wagon near some bushes, before he walks to a big stone, sits down on it and lets out a prolonged sigh.

Luzette moves towards the damaged doors of the cage and looks back down the plateau with her hand shading her eyes. The morning sun has been shining at their back since they passed the bend in the cliff. She then turns, looks past the colossus and stares into the distance, between the big boulders and bushes on the sides of the path.
The view from this treacherously high cliff is very impressive as the bright morning sun sparkles on the snowy, majestic mountains far away in the north.

The older giant turns around and looks at the girl and his brother.

He angrily stomps his foot, to get his brother's attention and points at the end of their path some distance further away, where the narrowing plateau simply seems to end.

His younger brother just looks up briefly and sighs, while he continues to eat a piece of dry meat that he brought with him. Just before he puts it in his mouth, his older brother grabs it out of his hand with a growl. He pulls off a piece with his dirty teeth and sits down on a stone as well.

The younger giant, obviously tired and annoyed, fetches another piece of dry meat out of his fur vest pocket and silently continues to eat.

As they pass the bend and see the giants further up, the knights stop and tie up their horses in a little grassy area behind some big boulders and a few trees, out of the giants' sight.

Kanoa carefully leads his horse to the other horses and looks over to the other side of the path. He watches how Keiji, Nabhitha and the guards also hide their horses. The boy also notices that Keiji instructs a guard to take a long rope off the horse.

Bo is still with Keiji but keeps his eyes on Kanoa, who crouches down a little and rushes across the open area to the bushes on the other side of the path, where the little black dog joyfully welcomes him. Kanoa squats down, pets the little dog and looks at Keiji. He points his finger further up the plateau, at some bushes and large rocks near the wagon, where Luzette is still imprisoned.

As Kanoa stands up and carefully watches the area, Keiji understands that the boy will try to reach the wagon by sneaking through the bushes and between the boulders. Keiji nods and bends down in front of Bo to prevent the dog from following Kanoa, which might give away his secret approach.

The boy crouches down and cautiously sneaks through the foliage, moving from large stones to bushes, behind trees and small rock formations. As he gets closer to Luzette, she notices Kanoa approaching the wagon and looks tensely at both the giants as they sit and chew.

Luzette watches him drawing closer, hiding behind some boulders and bushes behind the wagon. Then Kanoa slowly crawls toward the wagon, hiding behind a big stone nearby. Luzette tries to keep the giants from seeing him and moves a little in front of the cage doors, allowing Kanoa to work on the rope that is knotted around the doors.

The younger giant looks up, sees the boy behind the wagon and softly grumbles, just enough to alert his older brother, who immediately stands up in a rage and stomps towards the wagon. His ferocious expression and his wild, thunderous footsteps reveal that he is determined to capture and hurt the boy.
Luzette screams as she sees Kanoa step back and stumble against the big stone behind him. She turns her head and watches the terrifying giant reaching out his arms. Keiji is no longer able to control the little barking dog as Bo restlessly jumps up and starts running toward the wagon.
The colossus grabs Kanoa and lifts the boy high in the air. He roars loudly and obviously intends to smash him against the stone. The furious giant turns around however when he suddenly hears his younger brother yelling loudly and sees him hurrying over.

The little black dog sees that Kanoa is in danger and almost flies over the stones and grass. Then it jumps up, bares its teeth, and lands on the giant's foot. Instantly, it sinks its teeth into the giant's big toe.
The furious colossus screams and releases Kanoa, who falls down next to the wagon. The younger giant grabs the boy's arm, quickly pulls him upright and briefly looks into Kanoa's eyes.
Bo releases the giant's toe and runs away rapidly. Safely behind a stone, the dog turns around, looks at the giants and barks a few times.
The knights, hidden further back behind the bushes and trees, contemplate whether they should attack. King Eadwin turns to Keiji on the other side behind some boulders and sees him clearly indicating that they should stay hidden.

The king nods. He understands that their presence is still unnoticed and gestures to the knights to remain silent.
Keiji leads Nabhitha and the guards cautiously around the boulders and bushes, drawing slowly closer to Luzette, Kanoa, the giants, the crown and the marble.
As King Eadwin notices Keiji and the others slowly moving forward, he nods to his knights and they carefully close in on the wagon, hiding behind rock formations, trees and bushes.

The younger giant pulls Kanoa behind him when his menacing older brother tries to grab the boy. Kanoa shrinks and hides himself behind the younger giant. The larger colossus notices the crown resting askew on his head. He places it again on top of his head and breathes quite audibly a few times before he points at the wagon, turns around and starts walking up the last piece of the plateau.
His smaller brother sighs almost relieved. Silently he takes a rope off the wagon and binds Kanoa to the outside of the cage.
Luzette gradually sits up in the cage and looks at Kanoa, who just smiles somewhat apologetically.
He looks back at Bo. The little dog is still barking every now and then and restlessly walking closer to the cage and back again. The younger giant looks at the little dog and just smiles and sighs. Then he turns around, picks up the wagon handles and slowly begins pulling the cage-wagon again, following his older brother along a path that simply seems to stop further up the plateau. Bo still follows them but now seems to be bothered by his injured leg.

Keiji and the others follow as well but they keep a safe distance and remain unseen, as do King Eadwin and the knights on the other side of the path leading up to the top of the sloped plateau.
Just before the giants arrive at the edge of the cliff, the younger giant leads the wagon in front of one of the last large rock formations on the cliff. He parks the wagon in front of a steep stone wall.

The sharp, rocky end of this plateau consists of slightly sloping, flat light-grey shale and small strips of grass. Having arrived at the top, the older giant now holds the crown on his head with one hand and bends forward carefully to look over the rocky edge. He briefly looks down the cliff and sees a dark and seemingly infinite valley below him. The colossus angrily frowns, grumbles and then looks around somewhat desperately.

He turns around towards his younger brother and gestures for him to guard Kanoa, who is tied to the wagon, and Luzette, who is still in the cage. Kanoa sees the younger giant sigh and shake his head a few times before he walks over to the wagon. The malevolent colossus looks downhill with curiosity. Although everything seems quiet, he fetches the enormous whip in one hand and the big sword in the other, before he starts walking slowly down the plateau.

Seeing the colossus approaching, the little dog turns around and disappears into the bushes. This draws the attention of the colossus, who now begins to carefully look around to see whether the king and the knights have followed them.

He starts to swing his sword low, while he walks towards the right side of the path further down. Keiji, Nabhitha and the guards dive down behind some bushes. When Keiji slowly and silently draws his sword, the others noiselessly follow his example.

He gestures for them to keep silent and wait. He carefully squints toward the other side of the path, behind the giant, where the king shows himself from behind some boulders and nods. When Keiji hears the loudly breathing colossus closing in, he points at Nabhitha and a guard and subsequently to the left foot of the approaching giant. He then looks at the other guard and points at the other foot.

The guard firmly nods and Keiji sees that Nabhitha and the other guard stand ready. Keiji slowly stands up, lifts up his sword and, as soon as the angry colossus notices him, he jumps out of the bushes yelling loudly.

At the same moment, Nabhitha and the guards also jump towards the approaching colossus. The wildly roaring giant immediately swings his sword and Keiji and the guard are forced to dive down.
Nabhitha and the other guard also bend down but manage to swing their swords against the giant's ankle before they retreat. The giant screams horribly and watches Nabhitha withdraw into the bushes. While the giant is distracted, Keiji and the guard take the opportunity to strike him powerfully in his other foot.

While his screams pierce through the air, the giant violently swings his sword towards Keiji, who dives into the bushes as fast as he can.
Just before the heavy sword of the evil colossus hits the bushes, King Eadwin and the knights attack his legs from behind with their swords and manage to cut the straps holding the leather armor on his left leg. This attack causes the colossus to shriek wildly and release his sword. It falls down, smashes a bush and finally lands on the rocks right beside Nabhitha with a heavy clanging sound.
The wild and violent movements of the enraged colossus cause the king and the knights to step back. The colossus then looks down at the cuts in his injured left leg and feet and with a growl he turns around to his younger brother, who is watching the fight while he guards the prisoners. The wounded colossus slowly walks back towards his brother.

Luzette is still locked inside the cage, but with her hands outside the bars she desperately tries to untie the rope holding Kanoa to the wagon. As the huge colossus comes closer to the wagon, Keiji feels they must attack again quickly. He whispers to one of the guards who then hands him the long rope. He takes one end of the rope and ties it around his shoulder and torso.
He then looks at the guard, who immediately starts tying his end of the rope as well.

Keiji nods at Nabhitha and King Eadwin before he and the guard start walking fairly close together up the slope in the open, middle part of the narrowing plateau.
They approach the giants at an increasing pace. They are followed by Nabhitha and the other guard, who remain hidden between bushes and boulders on the right-hand side of the path.
To the left, the king and his knights also advance quickly toward the end of the plateau, hiding behind trees and a few small rock formations.

When the wounded giant has almost arrived at the wagon, the younger giant sees Keiji and the guard approaching rapidly and gestures for his brother to turn around.
When the angry colossus does so, he growls threatening and spreads his legs, pounding both feet, covered in blood, hard on the stone ground in the center of the end of the cliff.

14. Alone Together

Keiji and the guard increase their speed even more as they approach the intimidating colossus in front of them.
The colossus reaches for his whip but then he sees Keiji and the guard suddenly splitting up in front of him, revealing the rope between them.
As they quickly run past the confused giant on both sides, the rope presses against the legs of the colossus. Keiji and the guard pull the rope towards the edge of the cliff with all of their strength.

The angry colossus has to step back and almost loses his balance. But he manages to turn around and suddenly runs forward a few steps. This loosens the rope all at once and causes Keiji and the guard to fall violently to the ground.
The colossus steps over the rope, grabs it and viciously pulls it while running towards the edge of the cliff, violently dragging Keiji and the guard, still tied to the rope, over the rocky ground.
Before the high plateau ends, he suddenly stands still and yanks the rope with incredible force in order to swing Keiji and the guard, who are being scraped and rolled over the rocky ground, towards the edge of the cliff.

As Keiji and the guard almost tumble past the giant, he pulls and swings the rope over the cliff into the valley below. The guard scratches at the flat stones with his feet and his fingers to find some grip, but he is moving too quickly and rolls over the edge of the cliff.
The remaining rope inevitably follows the guard over the edge. Keiji desperately tries to find something to hold onto but he is inescapably pulled straight over the edge, into the dark valley below.

As Nabhitha watches Keiji disappear over the edge of the cliff, she screams with rage and charges at the malevolent colossus. She is instantly followed by the other guard, King Eadwin and the knights.

The big colossus turns and sees Nabhitha and the others holding their swords high and screaming as they approach him. He growls at his younger brother to get him to join in the fight. The smaller giant briefly looks at Kanoa and steps towards his raging brother, who swings back his large whip and raises his arm.

Luzette immediately continues her efforts to untie the rope that binds Kanoa to the wagon. Kanoa bends and twists his arms and finally manages to free himself. The girl removes the rest of the rope and drops it behind the wagon while Kanoa tries to untie the thick rope still holding the cage doors shut. As he anxiously works on the rope, Luzette suddenly whispers Keiji's name and points at the edge of the cliff.

It seems the rope between the guard and Keiji snagged a protruding piece of rock, leaving them dangling against the steep side of the cliff with the valley far beneath them.

Kanoa turns his head and sees Keiji frantically trying to climb back over the edge with one hand scratching at the stones. The boy immediately jumps up and rushes to the edge.

He grabs Keiji's wrist and, with a lot of effort, manages to help Keiji back onto the cliff. As Keiji lays down exhausted, Kanoa follows the rope, attached to Keiji and looks down over the edge. Below he sees the eastern guard, dangling above the valley, desperately trying to climb up the rope.

Kanoa starts pulling the rope. Keiji immediately stands up and helps him. When the guard finally reaches the edge, Keiji reaches out his hand and helps the exhausted man scramble over the edge. Keiji winds the rope, wraps it over his shoulder and just as Kanoa is about to return to the wagon, he hears Luzette. She screams anxiously as she watches the colossus raising his whip towards Nabhitha.

Then the boy sees Nabhitha, who was distracted by Keiji's return from the edge of the cliff, standing in front of the angry colossus. She is hit hard by the enormous whip, the end of which wraps itself around her torso.

When the colossus angrily yanks the whip back, Nabhitha is flung against a stone and then into the bushes. Her guard, the knights and the king run towards the roaring colossus with their swords raised. The younger giant, however, grabs a large, dead tree trunk and lifts it up high. With one swing he knocks the swords out of the knights' hands and smashes the tree trunk onto the ground in front of them.
The king and the guard jump back and evade the trunk. Just then Nabhitha, still a bit confused, crawls out of the bushes.

Luzette sees that the fight is going poorly for her rescuers and desperately turns to Keiji. Keiji looks at Kanoa, hands him his knife and points at Luzette before he runs towards the others.
Kanoa rushes back to the wagon and immediately starts cutting the thick rope on the cage doors with Keiji's knife.
Luzette anxiously holds on to the bars of the cage and sees Keiji draw his sword and run toward the bigger colossus from behind.
Bo suddenly appears between some boulders, next to the wagon. Kanoa notices the little dog in the corner of his eye, gives a rather strained smile and continues to cut the rope.

All at once, the ferocious colossus turns around towards his other attacker and raises his whip menacingly. Keiji does not run straight at the giants but agilely moves left and right to avoid their attack. The younger giant then picks up the big trunk and swings it over the ground, forcing Keiji to nimbly jump over it.
While the bigger giant starts swinging his long whip, Keiji dives past the giants through the legs of the older colossus. Since his whip cannot reach Keiji now, the evil colossus squints his eyes towards the wagon and redirects his swing towards Kanoa.

The boy is ferociously slammed against the steep rock wall behind the wagon. The vicious giant stomps towards Kanoa, who is dazed and trying to crawl towards the bushes.

Keiji gestures to the king, knights and guards to attack and distract the younger giant, before he starts running through the bushes to get behind the boulders next to the wagon.
Bo barks and runs behind some bushes, from there the little dog watches Keiji rapidly crawl towards a barely conscious Kanoa and grab his arm.
Meanwhile, Luzette screams loudly at the colossus, who was already bending down towards Kanoa. The colossus looks at her, frowns and growls annoyed. This gives Keiji and Kanoa just enough time to escape behind the boulders and follow Bo into the bushes.
The king, his knights and the eastern guards have to step back when the younger giant swings the trunk around in front of them. As they see Bo, followed by an exhausted Keiji and a recuperating Kanoa, appear out of the bushes nearby, they all look at each other and retreat together.
The younger giant now throws away the trunk and also steps back towards his angry older brother and Luzette, who is alone once more.

As the giants are now at a safe distance, Keiji and Nabhitha run towards each other, stop, stare for a moment and briefly embrace. King Eadwin grabs the handkerchief he received from Kanoa out of his vest pocket and looks at it once more intrigued. He turns to Kanoa, who is still recovering, and lays a hand on his shoulder, looking him in the eyes for some moments.
Keiji, Kanoa, Nabhitha, King Eadwin, the three knights and the two guards – hurt, but still standing – slowly gather in the middle of the plateau to keep an eye on the giants further away uphill. They look at each other with quite serious expressions and are clearly disappointed they have not succeeded in freeing Luzette, let alone capturing the crown and the marble.

The slightly wagging tail of Bo, the little black dog, standing behind Kanoa, seems to be the only happiness among them.
Keiji starts to gesture and points a few times at the plateau and the giants. The others closely watch Keiji and nod as he finally points at Luzette. They gradually start spreading out and seem to have a plan to rescue Luzette.

The elder giant now points at Luzette while he angrily looks at his brother, who is clearly once more obliged to guard Luzette. While Luzette sits in front of the cage doors, her hands are busy behind her back, pushing and pulling the partially cut rope, which still holds the cage doors together.

Keiji cautiously creeps forward through the bushes with the long rope on his shoulder again. While Nabhitha and the eastern guards follow him, the knights follow the king on the other side of the path, carefully hiding behind boulders, trees and bushes.
Kanoa remains in the open middle with Bo and scarcely looks at the terrifying giant as he approaches. When the colossus gradually raises his whip, Bo suddenly barks and runs forward. Kanoa just slowly walks forward. The others show themselves on the sides and it seems the final battle is about to commence.

While the younger giant stands close to the cage-wagon and Luzette, he sees that his older brother has stopped walking downhill and now stands ready to face the others, who now slowly approach.
The bigger colossus starts roaring with increasing intensity, his legs are spread wide apart. He stomps one of his feet on the ground a few times. He swings his whip around in the air once with one hand and then victoriously waves the golden crown with the other hand.
He puts the crown back on his head and holds his hand above his eyes. He watches as Kanoa approaches from further down the slope. The bright morning sun now shines straight into his eyes.

When he hears Bo barking beneath him, he briefly looks down and stomps his foot, causing Bo to retreat a bit. But the little black dog keeps annoying the angry colossus by barking around him.
Kanoa continues to slowly approach the giant while the others try to keep outside the range of the sweeping whip.

Suddenly Kanoa hears a crowing sound from behind and turns around to see Kra flying towards him from over the bend in the path. Kra's arrival is followed by an increasingly loud rumbling sound, which makes the horses standing near the bend very restless.

Kra lands on Kanoa's shoulder. The boy gently smiles and runs his finger over the rook's neck and looks back at where the rumbling is coming from. The young rook is now the only one looking at the malicious colossus, further away in front of them.
Even Bo is quiet and returns to Kanoa, as they all watch to see what is thundering around the bend towards them. As the horses behind the boulders and bushes start whinnying and restlessly trampling their hoofs, the ground starts to tremble. This makes even Luzette, who is still working on the thick, rigid rope around the doors, turn around.
She stands up as high as she can, until her head is pressed against the top of the cage. She slowly opens her mouth as she sees two huge rhinoceroses being lead by Zuberi. He gallops up the path on his graceful horse between the heavy animals. They are closely followed by two warriors and after them Zuberi's younger brother and Baaqir.

Luzette screams Zuberi's name as loud as she can, and it pierces through the air. Zuberi immediately yells her name in return and even increases their speed. The warriors begin to shout and wave for King Eadwin, Keiji and the others to move aside.
Kanoa moves to the side to make room for Zuberi, who now sees that Luzette is locked in the cage on the wagon close to the younger giant, further behind the threatening colossus.

Zuberi quickly turns around to both warriors and gestures for them to halt with the others. The warriors gradually come to a stop when Zuberi passes Keiji, the king and the others. They see his determined expression as he leads both rhinoceroses, pounding over the rocky ground towards the wagon.

Kanoa quickly rewards Kra with a little piece of bread before the rook flies off again towards an area with trees further down the sloped plateau.
The somewhat confused, larger colossus still holds his whip as he restlessly growls and watches the tall Zuberi leading the rhinoceroses straight toward him.
Zuberi yells something at the rhinoceros near the wagon, and slightly pushes his horse against the big rhinoceros, to make it turn towards the wagon. Zuberi then rapidly rides over to the other side of the plateau and has the other rhinoceros charge, head down, straight toward the bigger colossus.
The angry giant swings his whip towards Zuberi, who is rapidly approaching on his horse, but before he can strike, the rhinoceros plunges its horn into the giant's left leg and knocks him off balance.
While screaming dreadfully, the colossus bends at the knees and stumbles backwards. He drops his whip and holds the crown with the marble. Zuberi rides around the roaring colossus and calls to the rhinoceros to have him follow.

The young colossus near the wagon watches all of this and steps back when he sees the rhinoceros approaching him rapidly. Zuberi, now galloping towards the wagon, waves for Luzette to move to one side of the cage.
She braces herself in the far corner as the rhinoceros near Zuberi approaches and starts pushing against the backside of the heavy wooden cage, slowly cracking it open. While Zuberi gently tries to guide the rhinoceros backwards, its horn gets stuck between two bars. It swings its head a few times until its horn pulls off the back side of the cage, which then falls on the ground.

Luzette's bruised face shows a smile as she begins to climb out but Zuberi suddenly shouts at her anxiously because the other rhinoceros is now enthusiastically running towards the wagon. It hits the side hard, causing the whole wagon to shake. Luzette is thrown to the bottom of the creaking cage. Zuberi, a bit startled, guides the rhinoceroses further away. Luzette begins to stand up and grabs one of the bars. This makes another side of the cage crack and fall off. As Luzette screams somewhat startled, Zuberi returns and notices the top part of the cage threatening to collapse onto her.
Zuberi quickly pulls off the loose top with one hand, tosses it to the ground and stretches his arm towards Luzette, who looks at her savior happy and relieved.

The older and now severely injured colossus slowly stands up and roars at his brother, who briefly looks at Kanoa as he goes to assist his wounded brother.
Kanoa has been watching Zuberi's rescue and seems impressed. Bo, standing with the others further downhill, barks a few times and distracts the boy, who seems to be lost in his thoughts. Kanoa looks at the dog, smiles and then walks over to the others. Zuberi rides slowly over as well and is followed by both rhinoceroses. Luzette, sitting in front of him on the horse, leans her head against Zuberi's chest.

Both giants slowly retreat further up the narrowing plateau. The severely injured colossus stands before the edge of the cliff, turns around and sits down. The younger one stops near the damaged wagon. He seems to realize there is no reason to continue.

Kanoa wonders what King Eadwin and the others will decide to do, as Luzette is now finally free but the crown and the marble are still in the possession of the angry colossus. The boy sighs, bends down and pets Bo a little, before he looks up toward the edge of the cliff.
The irregular and almost constant roaring of the wounded and furious colossus almost seems to become a part of the whole environment.

15. Big and Small

King Eadwin is very relieved to see Luzette, who slowly dismounts Zuberi's horse. He takes her hand and guides her to the ground while Keiji rushes over to her.
They embrace each other tightly for a moment before Keiji looks at her once more and then turns to Zuberi, who stands in front of his horse and is warmly welcomed by his younger brother and his uncle Baaqir.
Baaqir is proud to see Zuberi's younger brother embracing and then bowing before Zuberi to demonstrate his sincere admiration and respect for his older brother. Keiji walks towards Luzette's savior and expresses his gratitude by quickly, yet forcefully, embracing him and happily patting him on the shoulder repeatedly.

Zuberi turns around and looks at the end of the rocky cliff, where the severely wounded giant seems to be resting at a safe distance.
The colossus angrily shouts at his younger brother, who is still standing in front of the damaged wagon and seems uncertain about what to do. He watches the crown fall off of his brother's head when he tries to feel his wounded left leg.
The colossus grabs the crown, puts it back on his head and grumbles one more time before he finally takes a look at the bleeding wound.

Everyone now takes a moment to catch their breath. Kanoa watches Keiji and Zuberi pointing at the rhinoceroses. Keiji hands his rope to Zuberi, who then walks rapidly towards the heavy animals.
They were eating grass and are now crushing and eating a few melons, which Baaqir brought with him in a sack.

Zuberi smiles at his uncle and gently lays his hand on the big horn of one of the rhinoceroses. As the huge animal looks up, Zuberi slowly slides his hand over its large head and starts tying the rope to the rings on the animal's leather collar.

Keiji walks towards Kanoa, puts his hand on the boy's shoulder and briefly smiles. The boy notices that Keiji's expression rapidly changes into a serious frown as he looks him in the eyes and then points at the sitting giant further away in front of them. Kanoa nods. Keiji walks over to King Eadwin and the knights. They are joined by Nabhitha and the eastern guards, Zuberi and the two warriors.
Baaqir guides Luzette and his young nephew to a safer area further back near the horses.

Kanoa sighs, bends down and pets Bo while he watches the others spread over the terrain and hide along the sides of this last narrow piece of the sloped plateau.
Zuberi, however, mounts his horse and Keiji hands him the rope tied to the rhinoceros. Keiji then looks at Kanoa and nods once firmly before he disappears into the bushes.
Standing up, Kanoa knows that he must proceed forward to attract the attention of the injured colossus, who is now gradually getting up. The giant firmly pushes the crown on his head and reaches for his whip.

Everyone is now ready for the final approach towards the end of the high, narrow cliff. Kanoa looks down at Bo and then steps forward, initiating their confrontation with the two giants.
The older colossus stands restlessly before the edge of the cliff. The intensity of his roaring increases and he leans briefly on his wounded left leg as he menacingly pounds his other foot on the rocky ground. The younger giant silently remains near the wagon and just watches his brother.
Kanoa looks at the angry colossus in front of him and slowly shakes his head a few times as he sees the desperation in the giant's actions.

Kanoa slowly, but steadily, proceeds and the others carefully follow him, still out of sight along the sides of the path.
Bo runs around Kanoa and regularly looks up, questioningly it seems. The boy stops, bends down, looks straight into the eyes of the dog and gently runs his hand over its head while trying to smile soothingly.

Kanoa stands up and sees the younger giant watching King Eadwin and the knights as they creep through the bushes at some distance behind Kanoa.
The young giant subsequently looks at the boy, the little black dog and at the boy again. Then he blinks his eyes and gives Kanoa a quick smile before he looks at his older brother further up the cliff. The boy notices this and silently continues past the younger giant.
He approaches the older colossus, who watches Kanoa's every move. The giant slowly starts raising the enormous whip he is carrying in his right hand while he holds the golden crown with the marble tightly on his head with the other hand.

Kanoa stops, remaining outside the range of the whip, and then suddenly holds his head askew for a moment. Bo turns around and barks once. Kanoa turns around as well and starts to smile. Keiji and the others do not yet seem to understand that the boy has heard the little black rook approaching.
And indeed, just a few moments later, the rook is flying towards them, followed by dozens of little birds, all gliding low above the ground.
Kanoa hears Baaqir, who is still hidden in the bushes, express his amazement when Kra flies straight at the boy, crowing repeatedly, followed by many small birds, which are now all twittering, chirping and whistling.

There is no fear in Kanoa's smile as he sees Kra and the cloud of birds swooping down towards him. Just in front of him they all climb back up towards the sky whooshing just over his head, blowing his hair backwards.

Everyone watches the young rook leading the birds higher up, passing over the annoyed colossus. Kanoa turns his head to see Kra and the cloud of birds, high above the valley, turning and then steeply diving straight towards the crown on the head of the staggered giant.

The colossus now turns towards the valley and holds the crown on his head with one hand and swings his whip with the other hand. The whip lashes out viciously but it is too low to harm any of the birds.
Kra lands on the crown and immediately starts pecking at the fingers of the loudly roaring colossus. Meanwhile, the other birds swoop around his face intensely flapping their wings and shrieking loudly. The colossus starts waving his hand in front of his face wildly and the rook immediately hops towards the marble on the crown and starts pecking at it. Then the little rook grasps the golden crown in its claws and starts to flap its wings.

The wildly moving colossus waves his hand above the crown and forces the rook to retreat upwards. All the other birds now start pecking at his face and as soon as he releases the crown to drive back the agile little birds in front of him, Kra and a few other birds start pecking the top of his head again. The ferocious colossus raises his other hand with his whip and thrashes it wildly above his head in an effort to get rid of Kra and the other birds on the crown.
The small birds quickly fly off above the valley before he strikes. However, the large whip in his hand does hit the golden crown, which falls backwards onto the ground.
As soon as the crown falls, Kra flies up into the air. The rook is quickly followed by the other birds, now turning around above the valley.

Kanoa watches the crown fall onto the rocky ground between him and the enraged giant, who immediately turns around loudly growling at the boy.
Keiji yells something and the others behind him all appear out of the bushes and from behind the boulders.

Kanoa now sees that the marble is knocked out of the crown by the impact of the fall. It darts through the colossus' legs and bounces towards the edge of the cliff they are standing on. Kanoa glimpses the approaching giant, who obviously did not notice the marble coming out of the crown.
The boy runs forward to grab the crown lying on the ground. He hears the others yelling and approaching as he snatches the crown, runs back rapidly and hides behind some boulders.
The young giant is still standing in front of the rock formation behind the damaged wagon. He presses himself against the steep wall of rock behind him as the king, the knights and the eastern guards approach him.

Kanoa turns his head just in time to see the tiny black marble roll over the edge of the cliff. Beyond the edge he sees only the wide valley and the snowy mountains far away to the north. As the cloud of little birds gradually scatters, Kra silently descends behind the colossus unnoticed and dives straight into the dark depths beyond the edge of the cliff.
The ferocious colossus now slowly limps towards Kanoa, who has the crown in his hands. The colossus sees the king, his knights and the guards closing in on his younger brother behind the wagon, but he now focuses on Kanoa, who is holding the crown and stumbling back against the boulders.

All of a sudden, Zuberi comes riding towards the furious, injured giant leading a rhinoceros while Keiji and Nabhitha also ride up to the colossus, one on each side.
Zuberi rides close to Keiji and throws one end of the rope that is tied to the rhinoceros to him. Keiji catches it and swiftly swings it back between the legs of the colossus, towards Nabhitha, creating a loop around the evil giant's leg. Nabhitha lithely catches the rope, immediately turns to Zuberi and throws it to him. Zuberi has already turned his horse and grabs the remaining piece of rope before he vigorously directs the rhinoceros and his horse back down the slope.

Nabhitha and Keiji retreat to the sides as the rope tightens quickly. The colossus furiously bends down and tries to grab the rope that is now tied around his already wounded left leg. But he is too late. Zuberi's horse tramples its front feet in the air and the powerful rhinoceros continues forward as they pull the rope until the wounded leg of the colossus is eventually pulled out from under him. Slowly he falls backward onto the ground.

Somewhat confused, the colossus leans on his arm and looks at his younger brother. He gestures taking back the crown from the boy while he turns his head toward Kanoa.
The king and his knights however have already surrounded the younger giant and he remains fearfully pressed against the stone wall behind him. Angry and in pain, the wounded colossus slowly sits up and reaches for the rope, wrapped around his leg.

Kanoa is hiding behind a few large boulders near the edge of the plateau. He is suddenly surprised by a soft crowing sound behind him and quickly turns his head to see Kra quietly landing on a boulder close to him. The boy's eyes grow wide as he sees the black, shiny marble in the rook's beak. The rook bobs its head up and down a few times.
Kanoa briefly looks at the colossus, who is still pulling on the rope on the ground. The boy reaches out his hand towards the little black rook, which drops the marble in his hand, once again. Kra immediately flies up and Kanoa quickly puts the marble in his pocket, takes the crown with both hands and looks at Nabhitha and Keiji on other side of the plateau.

King Eadwin, the knights and the eastern guards are close to the wagon. With their swords drawn they surround the young giant, who remains pressed against the stone wall. The bigger colossus in the middle of the plateau begins to stand up, still trying to untie the rope around his leg with one hand. With his other hand, he threateningly holds up the whip.

Kanoa sees Zuberi riding towards Keiji and Nabhitha and decides go over to them as well. He cautiously tries to sneak around the colossus, close to the edge of the cliff. But before Kanoa even reaches the edge, the big colossus furiously swings his whip towards the boy. The end of the whip wraps around Kanoa's leg. The colossus pulls hard and the boy is flung onto the ground. The crown bounces out of his hands and rolls downward towards the menacing colossus.

But then the crown rolls a bit off to the side. As the colossus tries to reach out for the rolling crown, Keiji yells Zuberi's name. Zuberi immediately commands his horse and the rhinoceros to pull again. Meanwhile Kanoa crawls towards the crown, which is now slowly rolling down the slope closer to the younger giant.
The older colossus shrieks as his injured leg is yanked backward again and he crashes to the ground.

Kanoa grabs the crown and hears the younger giant almost crying, backed against the stone wall, as King Eadwin and the knights push the points of their swords almost in his skin. When the frightened young giant desperately looks at Kanoa, holding the crown, the boy does not hesitate. Kanoa yells towards King Eadwin and shakes his head. The knights look questioningly at Kanoa while he slowly waves his hand, indicating that they should wait, and then shakes his head a few more times.
King Eadwin comprehends that Kanoa sees no purpose in hurting this young giant, who has clearly surrendered and only needs to be tied up for now.
As the king slowly retracts his sword, the poor scared giant looks back at Kanoa with a thankful smile.
Suddenly, however he looks behind Kanoa with a terrified expression and yells.
The wounded older colossus has managed to stand up and lashes his whip violently towards Kanoa. The whip wraps around the boy's chest and the colossus violently yanks it back, pulling Kanoa over the rocky ground closer to him.

Then he begins to slowly drag Kanoa towards the edge of the cliff.
Zuberi tries once again to pull the long rope with the rhinoceros but it seems he is too late this time. The colossus is prepared and braces himself while he drags Kanoa with one hand and forcefully pulls back the rope with his other hand, giving him more slack to proceed upwards, to the edge of the cliff. Kanoa screams while he slides over the ground still holding onto the crown.

Kra instantly comes flying out of a tree and starts bothering the colossus by flapping and loudly crowing in his face.
The infuriated, roaring colossus releases the slack rope and immediately strikes his fist hard against the little black rook.
The rook twists through the air before it slams against a rock, falls to the ground and lies still, close to Baaqir, who immediately steps forward and bends down to look after the poor animal.

Zuberi now approaches the colossus on his horse but suddenly turns to the side, revealing the two warriors behind him. They each throw a spear.
One spear hits the giant's right arm, causing him to drop the whip he was holding. This gives Kanoa the opportunity to loosen the whip that is wrapped around him by rolling backwards while still holding the crown. The other warrior's spear pierces the already injured left leg of the colossus, who groans in pain and sees Kanoa unwrapping the whip.
Zuberi rides back and has the rhinoceros once again pull the long rope that is still looped around the leg of the colossus.
As the tension on the rope increases, the colossus pulls the rope with one hand, grabs his knife and starts cutting the rope with the other hand. When the knife has almost cut through the rope, the colossus pulls the rope with all his strength. Zuberi and the rhinoceros react by pulling even harder.
Then the malevolent colossus abruptly releases the rope in his right hand and the rhinoceros flies forward.

The sudden increase in tension breaks the rope at the cut and the rhino subsequently stumbles forward downhill, falls and rolls a few times before it stops.
Zuberi immediately rides to the rhinoceros and inspects the animal, which is already standing up again. He also notices Luzette, his younger brother and Bo down the hill with the horses where Baaqir had guided them earlier. Since his uncle is now with Kra and the others up on the cliff, Zuberi swings off his horse and decides to stay with them. Luzette awaits him with open arms.

The colossus drops his knife and grabs his whip again. He stands, leaning on his right leg, before the edge of the cliff.
With a groan he watches Kanoa slowly standing up with the golden crown still in his hands. The boy cautiously covers the hole where the marble belongs with one hand.
Meanwhile, Keiji and Nabhitha assist the king and knights who have surrounded the young giant. Keiji ties his wrists to the handles of the wagon. When he briefly looks into the eyes of the cooperative young giant, Keiji understands that he will no longer be a threat.
As Keiji turns around he sees that the injured colossus is now standing ominously before Kanoa and raising his whip. He yells at the warriors to use their knives and attack once more. The desperate, wounded colossus pounds his foot on the crackling, rocky ground. He raises his whip and, just as Kanoa bends down quickly, the long whip sweeps over the boy, and cracks against the legs of the warriors. They both fall and grab their bleeding legs in agony.

Keiji, Nabhitha and the guards now approach but remain behind Kanoa, who stands face to face with the venomously angry but weakening colossus. Once more the giant stomps his foot on the trembling ground beneath him. Kanoa turns his head and briefly looks at Baaqir, holding the little wounded rook in his hands with great concern. The boy then looks up, straight into the eyes of the growling monster before him, and slowly starts moving his foot backwards, tightening his grip on the golden crown.

16. Into the Deep

Seeing Kanoa stepping back with the crown enrages the colossus even more, and he slings his whip into the air. Keiji shouts Kanoa's name and holds up his hands high.
As Kanoa turns around and raises the crown in order to throw it to Keiji, he feels the whip whooshing over and wrapping itself around his arms.
Barely able to keep hold of the crown, Kanoa falls and is dragged towards the evilly laughing colossus, who pulls in the whip and victoriously pounds his foot on the rocky ground again.

Kanoa feels how the ground beneath him shakes and then notices the increasing crackling sounds on the sides of the cliff they are on. While his hands still squeeze the crown, scratching over the ground, Kanoa tries to use his feet to grasp at anything he can. As Kanoa is dragged closer to the colossus and closer to the edge of the cliff, he sees the dark valley and the snow-capped mountains beyond.

While Keiji and Nabhitha run to Kanoa, the colossus, leaning on his injured leg, stomps his tremendous and bleeding foot on the last, trembling piece of the plateau, threatening the others from coming any closer.
Kanoa feels the vibrating rock under him and hears some loud, short cracking noises around him. Suddenly a large crack tears the rocky ground open right under Kanoa and spreads to the left and right side, around the colossus. The boy feels the rock under the crown trembling as this last piece of the cliff seems to be breaking off.
While his arms are still being dragged forward by the colossus, Kanoa feels Keiji and Nabhitha each firmly grasp one of his legs and start pulling him back.

The crack in the cliff bursts open right underneath Kanoa's shoulders. Finally, the endlessly roaring colossus is quiet and with a frown looks down as the rock he is standing on rumbles and slowly gives way underneath him.

Kanoa sees the giant silently look at him, at the crown and then at his whip, still tied to Kanoa's arms. While the cliff that the colossus is standing on collapses with a deafening rumble, Kanoa feels the ground under his arms and shoulders giving way as well. The colossus still holds on to the whip, which will eventually begin pulling Kanoa over the edge.

Keiji and Nabhitha who are holding Kanoa's legs start sliding forward and yell loudly while Kanoa watches the colossus falling in front of him, still looking at the crown.
He holds up his whip as he descends slowly and silently into the valley's depths. The eastern guards and tribal warriors grab Keiji's and Nabhitha's legs and prevent them, and thus Kanoa, from sliding further over the crumbling edge of the cliff.

At the palace in the east, the sultan stands near the sinister man, who is sitting at the table and refilling his cup. As he watches this vicious, perhaps even pathetic figure, the sultan doubts whether he made the right decision to invite the man in.
He slowly steps back and then walks to another room while he gestures for his advisors on the other side of the palace hall to follow him.
While the guards closely watch the sinister man, eating the last pieces of bread at the table, the sultan deliberates with his advisors. After a while, the sultan walks back to the guards having clearly made up his mind. He whispers some things to them and walks towards the courtyard.
Looking back, he sees the guards helping the confused man stand up. The sinister cloaked figure is now guided outside as well.

In the courtyard, the sultan points to a heavily guarded building that has a few small windows with thick metal bars and then looks back at the guards.

When the sinister figure realizes that he is being taken to a prison, he seems somewhat bewildered and just mumbles incoherently as he looks at the sultan, who has already turned away to give orders to the leader of a large group of guards.

The sinister man restlessly looks around but does not resist. He is led into the prison building and guided into a cell. As the guards close the heavy door behind him, the cloaked man walks to the small window in the thick stone wall. He grabs a metal bar with one hand while he leans on his walking stick with the other.

In the courtyard he sees the sultan and a large group of guards, all on their horses, lining up towards the gate and preparing to leave.

On the edge of the cliff, looking at the deep valley below, Kanoa sees the colossus falling and realizes that the giant's whip will drag him over the edge in a moment. His only chance to escape is to have the colossus release the whip immediately.

Kanoa looks down at the colossus and, just before the whip tightens, drops the crown toward the giant.

The colossus immediately reaches for the crown and in doing so releases the whip.

He snatches the crown out of the air triumphantly and falls further into the darkness below. The whip remains dangling from the boy's arms.

Kanoa feels himself being slowly pulled back onto the newly formed edge of the cliff. The boy is now able to unwrap the whip. Once it is unwrapped he lets go of the end and watches the whip plunge silently into the darkness of the immense valley below.

There are sighs of relief as Kanoa finally stands up.

Even the young giant raises his arms in celebration. By doing
so he accidently pulls up the wagon that his hands are tied
to. This startles the king and knights, who grab for their
swords again.
His apologetic smile eases their minds and the young giant
sincerely seems to be very happy and relieved, knowing that
his older brother can no longer threaten and abuse him.

They walk over to Baaqir, who is still holding Kra. Baaqir now
turns to the boy. Kanoa secretly feels in his pocket and
breathes a small sigh of relief to find that the marble Kra
gave him is still there. He leaves the black marble there for
now as he anxiously looks at Kra. Kanoa bends down and
carefully pets the poor creature, gently touching its feathers
with one finger.

Baaqir quietly holds the rook with one hand while his other
hand slowly lifts up a wing, which looks crooked and is
probably broken. Kra's eyes slowly open halfway every now
and then. Its irregular breathing indicates that the little black
rook is seriously wounded.
Kanoa sadly holds his finger under its beak and notices a
small drop of blood on his fingertip as he hears Bo running
towards him. Luzette, Zuberi and his younger brother silently
approach from downhill behind the dog. They see King
Eadwin, followed by the knights, Keiji, Nabhitha, the eastern
guards and the southern tribal warriors all quietly gather
around Baaqir and Kanoa, who is now kneeling down and
holding the badly injured little bird.

They are all suddenly startled by loud crashing sounds
behind them. Everybody turns around to see the young giant,
who is still tied to the damaged wagon dragging it with him,
as he anxiously tries to see what they are all looking at.
The last pieces of the damaged cage fall off the wagon as
the approaching giant pulls it rather awkwardly over the
rocks.

Keiji seems to understand that the giant means no harm, so he walks towards him and gently waves his hand to calm him down.

The giant restlessly sighs and watches how Keiji pulls off the remaining parts of the broken cage and proceeds towards the giant's right hand.

Keiji looks at him while he unties the rope around his wrist and smiles at the giant, who watches with amazement as one of his hands is released. Keiji grabs a piece of dry meat out of his pocket and presents it to him. The giant slowly takes it out of Keiji's hand with his free hand, throws it in his mouth and immediately starts chewing while he slowly closes his eyes.

After a short while, the giant looks rather seriously at Keiji before he lays his free hand on his large chest and respectfully bows before him. Keiji nods and smiles before he turns around to the others, who were silently watching.

As Nabhitha walks towards Keiji, the eastern guards follow her. The king and his knights prepare to return to the horses further down the slope. Zuberi sends the warriors downhill to bring the horses while he remains close to Baaqir, his younger brother, Luzette, Kanoa and Kra. Bo expresses his grief for the wounded little rook by softly howling and restlessly walking around them.

Baaqir mumbles something to Zuberi, who bends down over them. Zuberi immediately walks to the bushes and starts searching for something on the ground. He softly calls to his brother, who then searches with him beneath the bushes.

Kanoa, now holding the rook, gently runs his finger over Kra's feathers and sees how Baaqir slowly, almost creakingly, stands up. He fetches a piece of bread and a leather pouch out of his bag. He opens the pouch, drips some water over the bread and takes a softened piece between his fingers.

Baaqir kneels down carefully and presents the piece of bread to the rook.

Kanoa looks worried but hopeful as he watches the poor, injured bird slowly point its beak towards the wet bread.

He steers the bird's beak forward a little and watches how Kra weakly eats the bread.

Baaqir mumbles and smiles with relief as he turns around towards Zuberi and his younger brother, who return with several thin sticks and twigs in their hands.

Baaqir carefully inspects his robe and then gently pulls a thread from it. Then he looks around for a suitable place to treat the injured bird. Kanoa slowly stands up, cautiously holding Kra in his hands, and turns to the wagon.

When the young giant sees the rook in the boy's hands, his eyes grow wide. His mouth starts to hang open as he looks closely at the injured rook and then looks sympathetically at the boy. Kanoa nods towards the wagon, indicating that it could serve as a place for Baaqir to treat Kra's injured wing.

Zuberi immediately hands over his collected sticks to his younger brother, swings off his cape and spreads it flat over the wagon. When the giant and Zuberi briefly look at each other curiously, they share a sympathetic smile.

The giant grabs both handles of the wagon and steers it to a flatter area on the plateau and holds it firmly to keep it still.

Then he turns back his head and watches Baaqir carefully climbing onto the wagon.

Bo, the little dog, curiously runs around the wagon with a slight limp. Luzette steps forward, bends down and gently calms the little dog.

Meanwhile, Zuberi points at the rhinoceroses and looks at his brother, who promptly heads downhill.

Baaqir slowly sits down on the wagon, legs crossed, and lays down the piece of thread. He nods towards Kanoa, who hands the injured rook to Baaqir cautiously, climbs on the wagon, and sits down.

The boy watches Zuberi's uncle lay down the sticks and twigs close to the piece of thread on Zuberi's cape. Baaqir has Kanoa carefully hold the softly crowing bird. After he picks up a few thin, flexible twigs in one hand, he gently lifts Kra's wing with his other hand and takes a deep breath.

It is almost midday and the weak autumn sun slowly warms up the plateau. Keiji, King Eadwin and the others arrive at their horses, close to the bend in the widening path further down the plateau.

While Baaqir is meticulously fixing Kra's broken wing by supporting it with a few sticks, the others decide to take a break before preparing for the journey back. They fetch their bags and sit down on a grassy area.

Together they eat, drink, reflect and rest. Zuberi watches his brother direct the rhinoceroses to a grassy area further down the slope. After a while, the powerful animals begin grazing contentedly.

Suddenly, King Eadwin, who was quietly staring towards the wagon further up the hill, yells and points at the wagon.

They all look around to see Baaqir standing up and slowly climbing off the wagon. Kanoa remains on the wagon and holds Kra carefully against his chest, covering the little rook to give it some warmth.

Baaqir looks at the giant and smiles while he softly nods his head a few times. Then he waves his hand, indicating he wants the giant to bring the wagon still carrying Kanoa and Kra further down the hill to the others. As they proceed downhill they are enthusiastically followed by Bo.

Zuberi walks closer to Luzette and together they silently walk behind the wagon.

Before they reach the others, Kanoa briefly looks at the giant pulling the wagon and secretly fetches the marble out of his pocket. He holds it in front of Kra for a moment. The rook, still weak, slowly pecks the marble once and crows.

Kanoa immediately closes his hand when the giant looks back with a smile as he hears the bird. Before Kanoa puts the shiny black marble safely back into his pocket, he stares at it for a while and briefly smiles.

Baaqir instructs the giant to carefully bring the wagon to a stop but Kanoa remains sitting on the wagon with Kra.

The rook looks a little more alert now, but it obviously prefers to remain on Kanoa's arm, resting against his chest.
Baaqir walks to the others and fetches various pieces of food and fruit.
The others curiously watch how he takes all the food to the wagon and puts some of it in the back of the wagon, where the boy sits. The rest he puts in a corner on the front of the wagon near the handles to which the giant's left hand is still tied.
Baaqir looks at the others and is happy to see King Eadwin nodding approvingly. He starts slowly untying the rope around the wrist of the giant, who patiently waits for Baaqir to finish freeing him so he can finally eat.
Kanoa smiles as he sees the giant eating eagerly and the boy presents another wet piece of bread to the little black rook.

Baaqir sighs and sits down wearily. Zuberi follows Luzette, who sits down close to his uncle, but he notices his brother standing alone near the rhinoceroses. Zuberi calls to his younger brother, who hurries over to him. Then together, both brothers sit down close to their uncle as well.

The others all continue eating as King Eadwin slowly stands up and walks towards the wagon. As the giant sees the king approaching, he bows his head a few times, takes the last piece of his food and respectfully steps a bit away. He walks towards a tree, under which he comfortably sits down and continues to eat. Since the giant is now free, everybody keeps an eye on him.
But he simply chews his food with relish and only notices the others staring at him after he swallows the last bite. The giant blinks his eyes a few times and smiles. Then he closes his eyes, folds his hands over his chest and rests against the tree trunk with a satisfied and content look on his face.

17. The Walk Back

King Eadwin leans over the wagon and looks at the black rook, which is still resting on Kanoa's arm against his chest.
Kanoa looks up and smiles while his hand slowly brushes over his pocket, in which the marble is hidden, but he leaves the shiny black marble where it is.
The king also smiles, stretches out his arm, and gently lays his hand on Kanoa's shoulder. He taps the boy's shoulder a few times and points at Kanoa's horse but the boy slowly shakes his head and looks down at Kra.
Apparently, he thinks riding on the horse would not be wise for the fragile, injured bird. When Kanoa looks up, he sees the king nod and smile understandingly. King Eadwin turns around towards the knights, who are already proceeding to their horses, and instructs them to take care of Kanoa's horse as well.

Keiji, Nabhitha and the eastern guards stand close to their horses and seem to be preparing for the journey back as well. Zuberi mounts his horse and looks at the rhinoceroses, a bit further downhill, and then at Luzette, walking to the wagon. His younger brother notices this and smilingly waves for him to go to Luzette. As Zuberi turns his horse, his younger brother hurries over to the rhinoceroses to prepare them for the journey back.
However, Zuberi first rides to the knight leading Kanoa's horse. He stretches out his arm, takes the reins and guides the horse to Luzette.
When she notices Zuberi approaching on his horse, she looks up and smiles. As she steps toward Kanoa's horse, Luzette frowns a little at first but then happily takes Zuberi's reaching hand and carefully climbs onto the horse.

Zuberi slowly turns his horse to his uncle and looks at the wagon while he gestures some things at him. Baaqir seems to understand what his nephew means as he nods a few times and smiles. Baaqir steps off his horse and leads it in front of the wagon while Zuberi and Luzette slowly ride toward the others.

The giant steps back and holds the wagon on the side, enabling Baaqir to tie his horse to the wagon's handles.

Kanoa moves back a little to make room for Baaqir. The old man now slowly climbs onto the wagon, sits down at the front and takes up the ropes.

Before Baaqir instructs his horse to begin pulling the wagon towards the others, Bo jumps on and sniffs around a bit. The little dog then lies down beside Kanoa, who gently lays his free hand on the little dog's head.

As they reach the others, who are now all waiting on their horses, Baaqir stops the horse and the wagon. Keiji waves towards the king and bends his head a little in order let the king and knights commence and lead the journey back downhill. However, King Eadwin holds his restless horse back and looks at the giant.

The somewhat glum young giant has been following the wagon and seems unsure what to do. He looks at Kanoa, who watches Zuberi and Luzette riding to Zuberi's younger brother and the rhinoceroses.

The hoofs of the horses of Keiji, the king and the others restlessly trample on the ground as Zuberi halts before them and looks back at the wagon.

Baaqir sees the giant looking around and trying to decide where to go, now that he is free. The old man bows his head a little and gives the giant a friendly smile before he gently pulls the ropes and slowly leads the wagon past the others.

Zuberi and Luzette, followed by Zuberi's brother, both the rhinoceroses and the tribal warriors, start to ride their way back down the plateau.

King Eadwin and Keiji let the wagon with Baaqir, Kanoa and Kra pass before them. Just as the king intends to follow the wagon, the giant suddenly runs after the wagon and then closely follows it. Kanoa can hear his pounding steps behind them. He turns around and smiles as he sees the gentle giant following along.

King Eadwin follows the giant with the knights while Keiji, Nabhitha and both eastern guards close the procession, travelling back down the plateau. They all calmly ride along and seem somewhat lost in their thoughts.
When they arrive at the bottom of the sloped plateau, close to the bridge and cave, Zuberi halts and they all stop behind him. Zuberi looks at the cave on the other side of the cliff, and then turns to the giant.
As they all watch, expecting the giant to return to his cave, the giant sadly stares at the cave, shakes his head and looks down at the ground. Kanoa frowns as he hears the others mumbling and he feels sad for the giant, who seems to be afraid and obviously does not want to return to the cave.

The boy suddenly looks at the giant and yells excitedly. As the giant looks up, Kanoa taps his hand on the wagon he is sitting on and points at the cave's entrance.
The giant questioningly frowns but then suddenly smiles. He immediately descends the flat, carved stone stairs towards the bridge and rushes into the cave. Everyone mumbles curiously until they see the giant coming back out of the cave, hastily pulling the other wagon.

While the giant almost drags the wagon back over the bridge, Kanoa calls Zuberi and enthusiastically points at the rhinoceroses. Zuberi steps off his horse and helps the giant pull the wagon over the last flat stone stairs before they both proceed toward the rhinoceroses.
Zuberi's brother is smiling excitedly and stands ready with ropes near the powerful animals.
The giant looks almost ashamed as he obviously is not used to others helping him.

Zuberi steps towards him and motions for the giant to take a seat on the wagon. It creaks as he slowly sits down and looks at Zuberi once more. Kanoa and Baaqir see Zuberi's eyes meet those of the giant. They look at each other briefly and smile once more. Zuberi stretches up a bit to pat the giant's shoulder. He mumbles something at his younger brother and returns to his horse.

As Zuberi's brother gently guides the rhinoceroses forward, the wagon slowly starts moving forward and creaking even more. The giant anxiously grabs the sides of the wagon.

Zuberi and Luzette follow the giant's wagon. On the other wagon with Kanoa and Kra, Baaqir smiles a little and has his horse follow the giant's wagon too. Somewhat amused by this circus, King Eadwin, Keiji and the others slowly follow the wagons. Soon all gradually increase their pace and they begin galloping towards the barren wastelands.

While the giant fearfully holds on to his wagon, Kanoa is enjoying the ride, especially as he sees the little rook opening its eyes more regularly. While the wind blows through his hair, Kanoa presents another piece of bread to Kra, still nice and warm against his chest. But Kanoa also notices another little drop of blood, slowly emerging from the side of the bird's beak.

He sighs anxiously while he covers the bird with one hand and with his other hand he slowly pets the little black dog resting beside him in the corner on the wagon.

After they have been traveling for some time and the sun has moved more to the west, Zuberi increases his pace to catch up to his younger brother, who is leading the rhinoceroses with the wagon holding the giant. When Zuberi passes the giant, he smiles in a friendly manner and waves his hand.

The giant returns the smile, somewhat nervously, and dares to release his hand from the wagon just for a moment to quickly wave back.

Zuberi continues until he rides next to his brother, who is leading the caravan, and gestures for him to slow down and come to a stop before they reach the flat, open wastelands.
Baaqir, driving the wagon carrying Kanoa and the rook, slowly brings his horse to a stop alongside the other wagon, from which the giant now slowly and carefully descends.
Kanoa watches how the giant stretches his legs. The boy also sees that the others obviously intend to take a break as well as they all dismount their horses around the two wagons.

The little black dog wakes up as the wagon stops. It stands up, shakes itself, sniffs around a bit and then jumps playfully off the wagon.
Kanoa carefully lifts up the rook, which softly crows, and he looks into its blue eyes. Baaqir turns around inquiringly, looks at the boy and bends his head closer to see the rook.
The old man helps Kanoa slowly stand up and step off the wagon while carefully holding Kra.
Baaqir stands in front of Kanoa. Slowly and carefully he lifts up and inspects the rook's broken wing. He seems somewhat satisfied as he watches the boy slowly remove his hand enabling the rook to stand on Kanoa's arm by itself.
The injured wing hangs very low however and Kra seems barely able to lift it up. Kanoa carefully puts the wing in its place and then gently covers the poor bird, letting it rest against his chest again.

Baaqir mumbles a little, turns around, fetches his bag and walks towards his nephews. Meanwhile, the giant gradually comes closer to Kanoa, taking very small steps. He bows his head down and looks at the boy questioningly.
Kanoa nods with a gentle smile and the giant bends down further to look at the little injured rook. The giant is now very close to Kanoa, who has to resist stepping backwards, away from the heavily breathing giant. Kanoa's eyes grow wider and he holds his breath for a moment, until Kra makes a few soft crowing sounds. This makes Kanoa and the giant smile. When he hears Baaqir returning, the giant slowly stands up straight.

Everyone prepares for the ride over the flat wastelands. The rhinoceroses, wagons and southern warriors will travel in the middle, the king and his companions will ride on their side to the west, while Keiji, Nabhitha and the eastern guards will travel on the other side of the wagons.

Both Kanoa and the giant climb onto their wagons. Baaqir looks back to see whether Kanoa and the little rook are ready to go. The giant immediately grabs the sides of his wagon as Zuberi's brother begins to lead the rhinoceroses toward the vast, chalky plane ahead.
The early afternoon sunlight reflects off of the crusty, light-grey landscape they are traveling over.

The various rock formations and a few dead trees cast short shadows. This desolate place looks harsh and empty but is also filled with light.
While Zuberi's brother leads the rhinoceroses and the wagon with the giant, Zuberi slows down a little until he is riding alongside Baaqir's wagon with Kanoa. He bends down a little and mumbles a few things to his uncle while he points forward. Zuberi quickly turns around and smiles at Kanoa, before he gallops further up to his brother. Kanoa hears Baaqir chuckling, as he notices the speed of their wagon is increasing. Bo sits up and Kanoa carefully ensures Kra is safely resting against him.
While Baaqir keeps encouraging his horse to run faster, he comes up alongside the other wagon.
Zuberi swiftly proceeds alongside the wagons. He smiles when he sees his younger brother urge the rhinoceroses to accelerate as well.

Kanoa, smiling somewhat nervously, looks over at the giant, who is fearfully clamped onto the loudly creaking wagon, while he stoically stares in front of him.
As they accelerate, Bo's ears flap in the wind. Kanoa lays his hand on the dog's neck and turns to smile at Zuberi, who seems to be utterly enjoying this race.

As Kanoa sees the wagons and the riders on each side all traveling at high speed over the wastelands, he watches the horizon in front of them.

The mountains and forests gradually seem to emerge out of the distant haze in front of them.

When the mountains become clearer, Zuberi squints and races ahead, obviously looking at something in the distance. Suddenly he slows down and raises his hand.

After his brother stops beside him and all the others come to a stop, King Eadwin and Keiji ride up to Zuberi.

They follow Zuberi's pointing finger and see a dust cloud, still far in front of them. It seems to be rapidly heading straight towards them.

As a rumbling sound becomes audible, the horses become restless and Baaqir steps off the wagon to calm his horse. The giant carefully steps off his wagon as well and sighs with relief. But as he turns around and notices the approaching cloud, he frowns and grabs onto the wagon.

While Bo starts barking, Kanoa stands up and watches the cloud take shape as it comes closer. The king grabs for his sword as he is able to distinguish a large group of riders approaching at a gallop.

Keiji suddenly yells Nabhitha's name. As Nabhitha slowly rides up to the front, she recognizes the riders as eastern guards and immediately rides towards them at great speed. Then she stops in their path, yells something and raises her hand.

As the orderly group of eastern guards slows down and gradually stops before Nabhitha, the sultan appears. He dismounts and walks towards his daughter. Nabhitha jumps off the horse and, somewhat nervously, turns to her father to see him standing before her with open arms.

Keiji smiles when he sees them embracing sincerely. Kanoa, not knowing that Nabhitha is the sultan's daughter, seems somewhat confused as he watches her speaking with the sultan.

Then the sultan calls for Keiji, and Kanoa watches Keiji nervously ride forward. The sultan briefly waves his hand towards the guards, who immediately form a path for Keiji standing at attention in a line on each side.

Every eastern guard respectfully bows down when Keiji passes. Kanoa looks impressed when he sees a wave of bowing guards on both sides of Keiji as he approaches the sultan and Nabhitha.

Keiji briefly looks at Nabhitha as he nervously dismounts, to stand face to face with the sultan, who smiles and opens his arms.

After a short and firm embrace with Keiji, the sultan greets King Eadwin, Zuberi and his brother before he walks towards the wagons.

He looks at the giant, somewhat nervously, and turns to Kanoa, who bows his head and smiles, still holding Kra. The sultan slowly peeks at the young rook, smiles and nods at Kanoa. Then he walks back to the eastern guards, mounts his horse and shouts Keiji's name, pointing past the mountains at the yet-invisible palace in the east.

Keiji looks at Nabhitha, who is proudly smiling, and turns his head to look at Luzette, Zuberi, Baaqir, Kanoa and the king.

He holds up one hand, restraining his restless horse with the other hand and turns his horse toward the east. Keiji and Nabhitha wave goodbye to their companions. Keiji looks at her briefly once more before he lowers his hand. With a shout, Keiji and Nabhitha gallop away rapidly and they are immediately followed by the sultan and all the eastern guards. The whole group gradually disappears into a dusty cloud.

Kanoa watches King Eadwin, Zuberi and Luzette deliberate as Baaqir walks towards them.

The king will obviously go west with the knights and the rhinoceroses will return to the south with Zuberi's brother, accompanied by the warriors. The horses Luzette and Zuberi are riding on belong at the castle and it looks as if they will travel with the king back to castle in the forested mountains.

But first Zuberi walks with Baaqir back to the wagon where Kanoa is sitting. Zuberi bends down, lays one hand on Kanoa's shoulder, points ahead and pronounces Baaqir's name. He then points at himself and subsequently at Luzette while he mentions her name. After a short pause, Zuberi points towards the mountains in the west, where the castle is, and mentions the names of both Eadwin and AnZhiMu, who they assume is still at the castle.
Zuberi then quickly stretches his finger back towards the path in front of the wagon, back to the cottage.

Kanoa follows Zuberi's finger and looks at Baaqir who is smiling and nodding, as he sits down on the front of the wagon. Baaqir will obviously take him back to the cottage while Zuberi and Luzette will pick up AnZhiMu and Zuberi's horse at the castle before they return to the cottage as well.
Zuberi sees Kanoa nod in approval and he proceeds to the giant. Zuberi's brother waves towards Kanoa, who raises his hand and waves back.
Just then Zuberi yells something at his younger brother and watches with amusement as the giant holds on tightly as the rhinoceroses slowly start pulling the wagon further over the wastelands to the south.

Kanoa cheerfully waves goodbye to the sympathetic young giant, who holds on to the wagon tightly with one hand and quickly tries to wave with his other hand. Kanoa can hear Baaqir's gentle laughter as the giant quickly grabs the wagon with both hands again and flashes them a broad smile, holding his head a bit askew. Zuberi's brother leads the rhinoceroses, the giant and the tribal warriors to the south and they slowly disappear into the distance.

King Eadwin rides up to Kanoa's wagon, stops his horse, looks at the boy and smiles for a few moments before he respectfully nods and waves goodbye.
As the king proceeds towards the mountains in the west, he is closely followed by his knights, Zuberi and Luzette, who playfully waves her hand.

Kanoa waves back briefly, knowing that he will soon see them back at the cottage.

The dusty clouds of the galloping rhinoceroses, now far in front of them, have almost vanished.

King Eadwin, the knights, Zuberi and Luzette ride quickly towards the southwest, closer to the forests and mountains, on their way back to the castle.

Baaqir takes up the reins and commences the journey back to the cottage near the stream and the old willow, where Kra found the marble before sunrise early yesterday morning.

18. Arrival

Kanoa sits back and enjoys the wagon ride. Bo lays down beside him as the boy gently lifts the young little rook, which gradually seems to be coming back to life. Baaqir smoothly steers the horse over the last pieces of the wastelands as green grass and foliage gradually replace the naked rocks. The rock formations decrease in size and number while various green, yellow and brown trees appear along the horizon in front of the green mountains in the west and the far mountains in the east.

While Baaqir slowly steers the wagon towards the road between the trees, Bo stands up and starts walking and sniffing around on the wagon. Kanoa holds Kra in front of him to watch the little rook standing on his wrist on its own. One wing still hangs very low and the boy looks concerned about whether it is able to fly. He slowly fetches a small piece of bread out of his pocket and holds it before Kra. The little rook flaps its wings as it picks the bread out of Kanoa's hand. When it tries to reposition the piece of bread in its beak, the bread falls out onto Zuberi's cape, still spread over the wagon floor.

The injured rook flaps its wings, slightly blowing Kanoa's hair backwards, and jumps onto the wagon floor. Although the injured wing remains stretched over the floor, the little rook manages to stand up. It picks up the bread before Bo even has an opportunity to sniff it. Baaqir looks back and happily watches Kra finally eat the little piece of crumbling bread.

The bright afternoon sun highlights the countless nuances of green, yellow and brown in the leaves.

The grass, bushes and plants that the road leads them through give off a refreshing scent, a welcome relief after the dry, lifeless wastelands they are returning from.
As they pass the first farms, an old women, carrying a basket filled with fresh apples, curiously looks up and gives Baaqir a friendly nod. Kanoa smiles and waves his hand as they pass her. Then he sits back, gradually closes his eyes, inhales long and deep, holds his breath for a moment and then slowly sighs out the air. After a moment he opens his eyes and absorbs the somewhat familiar scenery around him.
The boy sits up when he notices that the rook is becoming somewhat restless. He sees that the wagon is gradually approaching the path near the stream.
Kra's anxiety is noticed by the little dog, which begins sniffing over the edge of the wagon with a wagging tail.

Just as Kanoa catches sight of the old willow tree on the other side of the stream, the little rook starts spreading its wings and the boy quickly bends over it.
Baaqir slows down the wagon on the path alongside the stream when they reach the fork in the road that goes up the hill to the cottage. Kanoa looks at Baaqir and gestures for him to stop the wagon. As soon as the wagon comes to a stop, Kanoa carefully steps off with Kra on his arm.

Kanoa notices that Kra seems to be drawn to the other side of the stream, where the old crooked willow tree leans over the reeds and the water. However, he doubts whether he should release the poor injured rook.
Baaqir looks at the rook seriously and slowly starts to nod his head. Kanoa raises his arm and pets the little black rook gently on its neck feathers.
The rook lowers its head a little, crows, hops, turns towards the seemingly alluring area around the old willow tree and spreads its wings.

Kanoa watches Kra fly weakly off his arm and just manage to flutter over the water.

The sticks Baaqir attached to support the rook's broken wing seem to hold and flapping laboriously with all its strength the injured rook just manages to clear the reeds.
The young rook then flies up and lands, rather roughly, on a branch of the willow. It must flap its wing for some time before it can finally stand, with one wing hanging low, on the branch of the willow.

As soon as Bo sees Kra flying, the little black dog jumps off the wagon and joyfully runs, still limping a little, over the hill towards the cottage.
While Kanoa worryingly stares at Kra, he feels Baaqir's hand on his shoulder. He turns around to see that Baaqir is trying to soothe him with a gentle smile. The boy turns around one more time to see Kra, the brave young rook, holding onto the branch, rather weakly and restlessly, while it tries to maintain its balance with its broken wing pressed against the branch.

Kanoa sighs and smiles briefly as he climbs back on the wagon and nods towards Baaqir, who silently and slowly steers the horse over the path on their way back to the cottage. Bo is already there and is scaring away a few chickens with his enthusiastic barking. Kanoa gently folds Zuberi's cape and puts it under his arm.
Baaqir slowly parks the wagon in an open area just before the cottage and curiously looks at the white and gray horse behind the cottage. Then with a smile he turns to the little dog scratching at the door with its feet. The old man slowly descends from the wagon and walks to the horse to untie it.

With Zuberi's cape under his arm, Kanoa climbs off, walks to Bo and bends down to calm the restless young dog. Despite his efforts however Bo keeps on barking. Kanoa slowly pushes against the door and, before it opens further, Bo slips through the narrow opening.
Kanoa slowly enters the cottage to see the little black dog running toward the other dogs in the basket.

The other young dogs gather around Bo in the basket, close to their mother. Bo pushes his head against his mother and softly barks. Since the big dog scared Kanoa yesterday morning, he does not mind that it now seems asleep. He smiles and looks around for his bag and cape, which he left there yesterday before they all went to the castle in the king's carriage.

When the boy looks at the corner, where his bag still lays, he notices the fallen mug and spilled tea on the table.

Kanoa frowns and shivers as he turns to the dogs and bends down before the basket.

Kanoa carefully moves his hand over the big dog and discovers that it is not responding to anything. Putting his hand carefully on its side, he feels that it is still breathing weakly. Kanoa sighs and looks worried. He slowly brushes his hand over Bo's back. The little black dog looks at Kanoa and suddenly jumps up. It sniffs around, walks to the other room and starts barking loudly.

Meanwhile, King Eadwin, the knights, Zuberi and Luzette have arrived at the castle. While Zuberi leads the horses to servants waiting near the stables, the king leads the others to the stairs. The minstrel is informed about their arrival by a servant and comes walking outside just as they are passing both the guards in front of the entrance. Happy to see them all back, the minstrel smilingly approaches and greets them.

When the king asks for AnZhiMu, the minstrel mentions Bo's name and points towards the cottage far away.

As the minstrel repeats AnZhiMu's name and points at the cottage once more, the king frowns.

Upon hearing this Luzette looks disappointed, ties her shawl and seems eager to return to the cottage as well.

The king also sighs and seems rather disappointed but insists that they all come inside and quickly calls for a few servants to look after Luzette's wounds.

After some time, they all sit at the table in the castle hall to have something to eat and drink. Luzette remains standing however, and anxiously looks outside through the open entrance.

After Zuberi stands up, nods at the king and walks towards Luzette, the others all stand up and follow them outside.

While they proceed to the courtyard and Zuberi walks towards Baaqir's wagon-house, King Eadwin has a servant bring back the spirited, dark-brown horse Kanoa chose last night. It seems to have recuperated from the ride and now paws the ground impatiently. The king helps her onto the horse and smiles to see how delighted Luzette is to once again ride the strong, noble horse.

Since Baaqir took his camel to the south this morning, Zuberi mounts Baaqir's gold-colored horse and joins Luzette in the courtyard with a smile.

King Eadwin wishes them a fine voyage home. When he yells the name of AnZhiMu as they ride off, Luzette waves and nods towards the king.

In the pleasant afternoon sunshine, Luzette follows Zuberi out of the courtyard, galloping down the path between the trees towards their home.

Near the stream, the little black rook sits in the old willow tree. It is still very weak and barely able to stand. It needs to flap its wings exhaustingly to reach just one branch higher. There it remains standing unsteadily with its broken wing hanging low against the branch of the tree.

Kanoa throws Zuberi's cape over his bag in the corner, follows Bo's barking and suspiciously proceeds to the other room. There he sees the little black dog barking at AnZhiMu, who is terribly pale and lying diagonally on the bed.

The incredibly startled boy softly speaks her name, leans over the pale and seemingly lifeless body and carefully grabs both her shoulders. Bo howls softly when she does not appear to respond. Kanoa shouts "AnZhiMu" and shakes her shoulders harder. She is unconscious and her pale body seems paralyzed.

Kanoa desperately pushes on her shoulders and screams "AnZhiMu!" as loud as he can. Then he immediately yells for Baaqir.

Baaqir, who had already heard Kanoa's screams, runs to the door and enters the cottage.
He immediately notices the spilled tea and the unconscious dog as he walks towards the room where AnZhiMu lies on the bed. Kanoa steps back and sees the old man, whom he has only known to be very calm, nervously looking at the pale woman and feeling her head, her chest and her neck.
He turns around, walks to the dogs' basket, bends down and feels the mother dog as well. Baaqir anxiously stands up and looks at the tea, spilled over the table. He cautiously dips his little finger in the tea and smells it. He waits a moment, mumbles some things and instantly runs outside as if to fetch something.

While Kanoa still holds AnZhiMu, he whispers her name. All of a sudden, she gasps, opens her eyes and takes another deep breath. Although the paleness of her appearance worries him and makes him feel somewhat uneasy, Kanoa is very happy to see that she is alive.
Out of nowhere, he decides to show her the black marble and instantly fetches it out of his pocket. When he carefully holds the marble before her in his hand, AnZhiMu shows a faint, relieved smile.
But then, with great effort, she closes Kanoa's hand with her weak fingers and makes a throwing gesture with her hand before her arm drops down on the bed again.

Somewhat bewildered, Kanoa silently puts the marble back in his pocket. He notices that AnZhiMu stares at him rather questioningly. Suddenly, the boy remembers that she is not able to speak and realizes that she must be curious whether Luzette is safe.
Kanoa smiles, nods and looks at her as he says the names of Luzette, Zuberi and Eadwin. He points his finger to the west while he tries to blink his eyes soothingly.

AnZhiMu weakly smiles once more but keeps staring at him somewhat expectantly, as her breathing seems to weaken.

Kanoa suddenly smiles, a bit ashamed, and quickly mentions her son's name, Keiji, and points in the other direction, towards the east.
This seems to satisfy the poor woman and she smiles with genuine relief at Kanoa. She slowly grabs the boy's hand and moves it against her cheek.
AnZhiMu tries to smile before she closes her eyes and falls back into a deep unconsciousness.

As Kanoa turns around he notices an anxious Baaqir, who has just come in. Baaqir approaches the bed and nervously tries to decide what he should do. He holds several little flasks in one hand and his bag in the other. Baaqir slowly sits down on the bed and feels the woman's head again.

The boy turns around. He slowly and silently walks to the dogs, bends down and pets the young dogs a little. While the other young dogs remain with their unconscious mother, Bo jumps out of the basket and follows Kanoa as he stands up and walks over to his bag in the corner.
He looks at Zuberi's cape, thrown over his bag, and stares for a moment. He does not bend down, but turns to the door and walks outside, followed by the little black dog.

Kanoa slowly walks to the old ruins, where he woke up yesterday morning to the crowing sounds of Kra, and sits down on a big boulder. He enjoys the serenity of the autumn afternoon and closes his eyes to the slowly lowering sun for some moments.
When he slowly opens his eyes, he turns to the old willow tree and searches for the young rook, but he cannot see any sign of the rook from where he sits.
As he stands up, he turns to the mountains and distinguishes two riders quickly approaching. He squints and sees that it is Zuberi and Luzette returning from the castle.

He leans on the boulder with one hand and reaches over to gently pet Bo, while the little dog joyfully sniffs his arm and wags its tail.

The boy looks at the two returning riders once more, stands up and walks back to the cottage, a bit hastily.

When he enters the cottage, Kanoa looks into the bedroom and sees Baaqir, slightly sweating, still nervously trying to help AnZhiMu.
Kanoa sighs, picks up Zuberi's cape and puts it on a chair. He lays the cloak he got at the castle over another chair and bends down again to pick up his bag and his own cape. He turns around and walks to the bedroom, to AnZhiMu and Baaqir.
He quietly puts down the bag, slowly puts his cape over his shoulders and proceeds to the side of the bed. The little dog seems to follow every step Kanoa takes, as the boy silently kneels down and puts both his hands on the bed.

He looks at Baaqir, points towards the mountains, mentions Zuberi and Luzette and points briefly at his own eyes. The old man nods as he understands that his nephew and Luzette are approaching.
Kanoa carefully lays his hand over the cold, pale hand of AnZhiMu, who is still dressed in the shiny blue dress she wore at the castle yesterday. As the boy whispers her name once more, Baaqir looks at him. The old man looks sad and tense, yet he manages to smile soothingly at the boy. Kanoa takes AnZhiMu's hand with both his hands and calls her name one more time.

It is in vain it seems and Kanoa takes a deep breath, waits a moment, and then sighs. He runs one hand briefly over Bo's head and slowly stands up, picking up his bag with the other hand. Baaqir rises with him and seems to understand that the boy feels a certain urge to leave.
The frail old man steps in front of Kanoa and puts his hand on the boy's shoulder. Kanoa drops his bag and embraces him.

While Kanoa stares at the gravely ill AnZhiMu for another moment, Baaqir bends down and pets the little dog.

Baaqir slowly stands up, turns to the pale and unconscious woman on the bed and continues his desperate efforts to save her.
Kanoa walks to the other room with his bag and proceeds to the door, where he turns around to see Bo sniffing the other young dogs. The boy softly pronounces Bo's name and the little black dog immediately runs to Kanoa, now stepping through the doorway.

19. Dusk

With a troubled mind, Kanoa slowly walks to the path's junction close to the old tower ruins.
As he proceeds, carrying his bag, Bo is always around him. When they arrive at the ruins, Kanoa drops his bag and looks towards the mountains. The boy can see the two horses approaching over the path through the trees.

As Kanoa waits for Luzette and Zuberi, he sits down and absorbs his surroundings once more. He stares at the old willow tree, further down near the stream. He is not able to see Kra, the injured young rook, still weakly leaning on a branch, too unstable to sleep and almost too exhausted to hang on.
The rook's eyes are half closed and every now and then it looks below, to the spot on the ground beneath the tree, where it pulled the marble out of the ground yesterday at dawn.

Bo sniffs around in the ruins and inquiringly looks at Kanoa when he stands up and turns around towards the path near the stream.
Kanoa watches Zuberi and Luzette as they approach. The little dog restlessly stands behind the boy when it hears the horses approaching.
As Luzette and Zuberi steer their horses up the path to the ruins and see Kanoa waiting with Bo, they smile and wave.
Bo runs towards the horses and joyfully barks as Luzette stops her horse and dismounts.
Her smile fades as she sees Kanoa's bag behind him. She understands that his path does not end here. She turns her bruised face a bit askew and looks at him.

Then she briefly embraces Kanoa while the little dog wags its tail around them. Zuberi dismounts the gold-colored horse and watches Luzette bend down and pet Bo for a while. He also notices Kanoa's somewhat subdued smile.
Luzette stands up, turns to Kanoa, smiles, sighs and waves her hand at the playful dog once more.
Then she questioningly looks at Kanoa, asks about AnZhiMu and looks at the cottage. Zuberi watches how Kanoa shakes a little as he hears AnZhiMu's name and briefly points to the cottage.
Luzette lays her hand on Kanoa's arm for a moment, smiles once more and walks back to her horse. She joyfully leads it past them over the path toward the cottage and waves back one more time.

Kanoa turns to Zuberi, who smiles and lays his hand on the boy's shoulder as Kanoa is about to get his bag.
The boy first nods once, then looks down and sighs. When Zuberi curiously asks him about AnZhiMu he slowly shakes his head. Zuberi sees the troubled look on Kanoa's face as the boy looks at Luzette, still leading her horse toward the cottage.
Kanoa points at the cottage briefly and mentions Baaqir's name. As he turns back and looks up to Zuberi, he sighs.
The boy looks at his companion and slowly stretches out his arm to lay his hand on the shoulder of Zuberi, who sighs and pulls the boy closer in order to fully embrace him.

After a few silent moments, Zuberi looks at Bo, smiles and walks to his horse. Kanoa picks up his bag and watches the little black dog move aside for Zuberi's horse. He looks up at his friend as they both wave.

Luzette has just arrived in front of the cottage and leads the horse around the back. As Zuberi passes the ruins and turns to the path towards the cottage, Kanoa looks at the dead, old willow tree and walks slowly down towards the stream. Bo faithfully accompanies the boy.

Kanoa stops on the path junction, close to where the old, crooked weeping willow stands on the opposite side of the stream.
He puts down his bag near a big rock and looks back at the cottage, where Luzette awaits Zuberi, who is leading Baaqir's gold-colored horse to the other horses.

In this serene autumn afternoon Kanoa listens to the streaming water, the wind through the trees and a bird further away. He briefly looks at the old willow tree before he turns to the cottage once more and watches Luzette and Zuberi go inside.

The expression on Kanoa's face reveals that he feels sorry for the girl, who will probably soon find AnZhiMu on the bed just as he did.
He turns his head to the tree Kra had flown to earlier, but he barely has a moment to look for the rook before a piercing and heartbreaking scream shatters the stillness of the slowly approaching evening.
As Luzette's scream fades away, the boy hears some startled little birds fly up. He frowns and swallows while he slowly turns his head to the cottage.

Kanoa did not see the injured young rook lose its balance when Luzette screamed.
Startled and weakly crowing, it flaps its wings and falls. Kra bounces onto a lower branch, loses one of the sticks supporting its wing and breaks another stick.
The broken wing snaps as the poor little bird strikes the lowest branch before it falls to the ground beneath the willow tree, very close to the spot where it found the marble.

A breeze makes the autumn leaves rustle and Kanoa shivers. He ties his cape around his neck while he looks at the willow tree.
He is not able to see behind the long grass, where the weak and severely injured young rook crawls through the leaves, so close to where it found the marble yesterday at dawn.

Kanoa looks at the cottage but sees no movement except for the chickens, the cow and the swishing tail of one of the horses. He feels in his pocket and fetches the marble. He holds the little, black, shiny marble between his thumb and index finger while he stares at it.

Kanoa softly smiles as he then looks at the old, crooked tree. He seems to remember the little rook showing him where it found the marble under the willow tree when he came back from the village yesterday.
Suddenly he frowns and looks at the cottage for a moment, obviously thinking of how AnZhiMu, weak and barely conscious, gestured that he should throw away the marble when he showed it to her.

Kanoa turns his head towards the cottage again and notices that the others remain inside. The boy sighs and stares at the shiny marble again for quite some time.
The boy then closes his hand, crouches down next to Bo and smiles at his new loyal friend.
Kanoa rises, turns towards the tree, takes a deep breath and throws the black shiny marble over the stream.

It lands, bounces and comes to a stop right before Kra. The almost unconscious rook lying on the ground is startled by the shiny marble, rustling through the leaves in front of its beak. It opens its beak but it lacks even the strength to crow. The young rook flutters slightly on the ground and stretches its legs to shuffle a tiny bit towards the marble.
Kanoa watches the marble drop behind the reeds and grass, somewhere under the old tree.
He softly says Kra's name, but he cannot see the young rook struggling over the ground.

The boy turns around when he hears his name. He sees Zuberi and Luzette, coming out of the cottage.
Luzette leans her head against Zuberi's chest and Kanoa is pleased to see Zuberi supporting her with his arm around her back.

Baaqir comes rushing back from the horses with a small bag in his hand. Just before he disappears into the cottage, he waves to Kanoa with his other hand.
Though Luzette is exceptionally sad, she manages to smile briefly and wave goodbye to Kanoa, who just holds up his hand, like Zuberi does.
Kanoa slowly reaches for his bag as Zuberi gently helps Luzette back into the cottage. Zuberi holds up his hand one more time before he closes the door.

Kanoa watches the sun slowly reach the tops of the highest trees on the mountains in the west and he stares at the castle on the mountain far away for a moment.

The boy sighs and lifts his bag. He is still unable to see Kra, the badly injured young rook, approaching the marble with all the strength it has left.
The rook opens its beak, but it is still just a little distance away from the shiny black marble. This distance seems infinite to the weakening rook, and it now lies still on the ground, as its strength begins to fade away.

Kanoa tightens his cape and looks around for a path that he has not walked before. He looks up once more at the branches of the willow tree, hoping to see the brave young rook.
On the ground Kra stretches its legs and its neck, holds its beak open and flaps its wings in a final effort to obtain the marble one more time.

The boy softly speaks Kra's name again but cannot see how the rook at last manages to pick up the shiny marble in its beak.
It weakly shakes its head a few times over the ground, gags slightly and finally manages to lift its head and swallow the shiny black orb.
Relieved, and somewhat content it seems, the rook slowly closes its beak and its eyes.

It swallows once more before it crows very softly. The rook's head then slowly lowers until it lies still on the ground.
Its half-open eyes gradually close and hide their blue color.

Bo softly howls and looks up at Kanoa, who pronounces Kra's name softly one more time as he looks over the stream. When he lifts his bag and slowly starts walking, he briefly looks back to the cottage once more.
The sun shines at his back for now, but it is uncertain where the path will take them. It winds between the trees and hills in the distance toward an almost dusky horizon.

A soft autumn breeze rolls a few colorful leaves over the ground underneath the old willow tree.
One leaf tumbles over the rook and lands on its broken wing, another leaf rolls over the ground and stops against its motionless body.

The low sun casts the shadow of the mountains over the ground near the stream. It grows darker under the tree as the shadow surrounds the still body of Kra.
Two dragonflies pass the rock in the water, close to the reeds under the old tree. A bird chirps from a distance.
The buzzing sound of a fly, irregularly circling over Kra's body briefly interrupts the serenity around the young rook.
As dusk falls, Kanoa follows the path, now bending behind the hill along the stream. His loyal, young companion seems to walk joyfully after its lengthening shadow.
Just before the cottage, the old ruins and the willow tree are about to disappear from his sight, Kanoa stops, turns around and slowly squats down next to Bo.

While he softly pets the young dog's head, he drops his bag and shields his eyes with his other hand.
He looks one more time at the castle, the mountains, the hill, the cottage and the old willow tree near the stream in the distance.

His mind obviously wanders back to all the events that happened since yesterday morning, when he woke up to the crowing of Kra.

The expression on his face varies. He gently smiles and then frowns. Finally there is sadness. He lets out a prolonged sigh and then slowly stands up and fetches his bag.

Kanoa stares at the horizon before him for a while, looks at Bo and takes a deep breath. The faithful, young dog wags its tail happily and barks softly while it awaits the boy's next step.

The boy smiles at the young black dog and he continues walking on the winding path, wherever it will lead them.

While the young dog enthusiastically runs and sniffs around the boy, they gradually fade away behind the trees.

The colorful leaves softly rustle and a few gently float down through the calm and quiet air.

Under the old willow tree, in the increasingly dark shadows, the wind blows some more leaves over the rook on the ground. They gradually cover the young bird and it slowly becomes part of its surroundings.

The setting sun slowly sinks behind the many trees spread over the mountain in the west. The moon and stars emerge, but are still faint and far beyond the dusky horizon in front of the boy and the dog.

KRA

www.ingramcontent.com/pod-product-compliance
Lightning Source LLC
Chambersburg PA
CBHW020950180626
46814CB00003B/1018